# THE SPANIARD'S
# SURPRISE
# LOVE-CHILD

# THE SPANIARD'S
# SURPRISE
# LOVE-CHILD

KIM LAWRENCE

MILLS & BOON

First published in Great Britain 2020
by Mills & Boon, an imprint of HarperCollins*Publishers*
1 London Bridge Street, London, SE1 9GF

Large Print edition 2020

© 2020 Kim Lawrence

ISBN: 978-0-263-08479-5

**MIX**
Paper from
responsible sources
**FSC˚ C007454**

This book is produced from independently certified
FSC™ paper to ensure responsible forest management. For
more information visit www.harpercollins.co.uk/green.

Printed and bound in Great Britain
by CPI Group (UK) Ltd, Croydon, CR0 4YY

# CHAPTER ONE

THE CLASSICAL MUSIC playing through the sound system—gifted by a famous old girl after her first platinum album—was almost drowned out by the combined din of young voices, the shuffle of feet and the scraping of chairs on the ancient wood floor as uniformed pupils filed into the school auditorium.

Though several of her colleagues were frowning at the noise levels, Gwen barely noticed the racket that echoed off the high rafters of the school's Tudor hall. Her thoughts were wandering, though not far. The crèche—which had been the deal clincher when she was offered the job at Mere Grange—was not five hundred yards from where she was sitting beside the rest of the staff on the stage.

Despite a disturbed night that had made Gwen fear the worst, Ellie had seemed fine this morning. True, she had been a bit clingy when Gwen had dropped her off in the crèche earlier but her temperature had been normal. Gwen had checked it twice, but still the vague anxiety lingered. Was it maternal instincts or just guilt?

The former she'd always assumed to be an urban myth but she was now certain really did exist, and the latter, though she knew it was irrational, she had come to appreciate as a fact of life. Was it just her or perhaps single mums or maybe all mums? She couldn't be the only mum who felt that guilty tug every time she left her child in the crèche. For some reason even knowing that Ellie was well cared for and happy there didn't lessen the feeling.

'She'll be fine. Stop fretting.'

Ellie turned to her friend Cassie, the head of English, with a rueful smile. 'How did you know I was worrying about Ellie?'

'Love, you're always worrying about Ellie. You make parenting look easy but it must be tough doing it all alone.'

Gwen brought her lashes down in a protective sweep that shadowed her blue eyes. She had opened up more to Cassie than anyone else, but the other woman still only knew the bare minimum—just that Ellie's father was not English and he was not in the picture.

Her slender shoulders lifted in a shrug as she pushed away the image of Ellie's father that had slipped through the mental barriers she had erected, though, as she thought of him every single time she looked into her daughter's beautiful eyes, it hardly seemed worth the effort.

Before she could be drawn into an internal debate on her past mistakes and awful taste in men—or at least *one* man—a shout emanating from just below the stage made her turn her head.

The same noise had caught Cassie's attention.

'I'll have to go and help,' Gwen said after a moment. Her classroom assistant, Ruth, was struggling to contain the energy and boredom of a class of twenty five-year-olds who, thanks to someone who hadn't considered their lack of attention span, had been seated first in the auditorium.

'Good luck,' Cassie breathed, tacking on a low-voiced warning. 'The head will notice you're not sitting here with the rest of us and he won't be pleased. He said "*all* staff",' she quoted, adopting the man's distinctive clipped delivery.

'I doubt if one less bowed head is going to stop Lady Moneybags donating the money for the library extension. Anyway, he'd *notice* a lot more if one of my lot escapes—now that would make a bad headline.'

Gwen reached the front row just in time to cut off an adventurous member of her class before he slipped through a fire exit.

'This way, Max,' she said, touching the top of his curly red hair before she firmly took his hand and led him back to his seat. 'Oh, you're sitting next to William…*not* such a good idea.' A fact that Gwen had learnt the hard way, and in class she now had them sitting on opposite sides of the classroom. 'Move over, Sophie. Max can sit next to you. Excellent, now don't move,' she admonished, before moving down the row to where Ruth was sitting. 'You almost lost one there.'

'Sorry, Miss Meredith,' Ruth said, smiling her gratitude.

Gwen smiled back, though it never made her feel anything but ancient to be called Miss by the young woman who was actually a year older than her. The prestigious fee-paying school was very keen on defined roles and did not encourage use of Christian names in the professional setting or, for that matter, romantic relationships between staff, although blind eyes were turned so long as people were discreet.

Gwen wasn't interested in being discreet; she was simply not interested at all. In the odd quiet moment she wondered if her libido was dead, but not for long. Those moments were rare and the rest of the ninety-nine per cent of the time she was too exhausted to even think about it.

Even had she trusted her own judgment with men after her experience with Ellie's father, romance was a pretty low priority for her these days. Now sleep, and maybe finding a few more hours in a day to sit down and read a book or do her nails—these were the things she lusted after. Gwen had well and truly left physical lust behind and she didn't miss it one bit.

'No harm done, Ruth.'

'Max is pulling faces at me, Miss,' Sophie complained.

*'Max!'*

Gwen's glance moved over the red head of the culprit, who was now looking angelically innocent as she scanned the faces of her charges occupying the first two rows, waiting until she had their attention before she widened her eyes and raised a finger to her lips. The result was nothing approaching calm, but the imminent possibility of someone swinging from a chandelier or making an escape bid receded.

'It's a miracle!' she heard Ruth breathe. 'How do you do it?'

Gwen rewarded her charges with a nod of approval and, more importantly, promised them a nature walk because they were being so good. She usually found the carrot a lot more effective than the stick. But before she could make her way back to the stage, the sudden lowering of the hum of youthful voices in the room indicated that she was too late to slip unobtrusively back to her seat, so instead she sat down on the bench next to Ruth as the head walked on the stage with their VIP guest speaker.

The head had a voice that filled the auditorium without effort and silence immediately fell. Barely listening to the introduction, Gwen kept her attention on her pupils, while hoping the guest speaker didn't turn out to be as fond of the sound of their own voice as the head. A five-year-old's attention span was limited, especially when they were bored, but hopefully they would fall asleep rather than run amok.

'And now I give you Mr Bardales.'

*Bardales...* No, surely it was the *Cavendish* Prize that was being given by the benefactor that the new science block was named after? *Bardales* was a very different name with very different connotations for Gwen.

On the surface nothing changed. Outside she was a serene swan, with only the fluttering of the long curling lashes that framed her sapphire-blue eyes and the faintest quiver of the fine muscles beneath the skin around her wide mouth betraying that under the surface she was frantically duck paddling to stay afloat, a heartbeat away from...*who knew*? Total panic? She'd never gone there and she never intended to—it was all a matter of control.

*Breathe, Gwen*, she told herself. The breath left her parted lips in a slow, uneven, near-silent hiss as, like someone who had jumped in the deep end of the pool by accident, she kicked for the surface, leaving panic behind.

She brushed her forearms hard with her hands, rubbing the rash of goosebumps that had broken out over her skin. She despised her stupid overreaction, the first in a while. It had to have been a couple of months ago the last time she had experienced the dry-throated, heart-racing sensation of stepping off a cliff in the pit of her stomach. On that occasion it had been triggered when she'd seen a dark head standing out from the crowd in the middle of the busy shopping centre, but a moment later she had realised there was no definitive arrogant angle to his jaw, no big-cat fluidity to his stride. The sensation hadn't lasted longer than a moment before her common sense reasserted itself and was followed by the sigh of relief that left her feeling foolish and annoyed with herself for allowing her overactive imagination to take control, even for a second.

The annoyance with herself was already kicking in hard as she tipped her head back to see the cause of her flashback. She had to tip it back some more as the guest was tall, the cut of his dark suit not disguising the power of his lean muscle-packed frame.

No, it hadn't been a flashback; *this* was a flashback! And pulling free of it was not an option. Nearly three years suddenly slipped away and she was back in New York.

The bar was as cool and sophisticated as its clientele and Gwen, sitting perched on a tall stool, fitted right in; she was cool, she was sleek and she belonged...or at least she *looked* as though she did and that was what counted, she'd discovered. She imagined there would be a time when it didn't feel as though she were playing a part. It would come; she'd only been in New York three months and she knew it couldn't happen overnight. She focused instead on the positives, the most positive aspect being that her five-year plan was already off to a flying start.

The first month at work she'd been finding her feet, so anxious to make a good impression that she had been unable to hide it. She did what she'd done all through university, when she had known that if her plan was to succeed she needed a good degree—some people could party and still get good results, but Gwen knew she couldn't do that; she had to focus solely on work. So she kept her head down, sacrificing a social life to achieve what she needed. It had taken her a few weeks before she'd realised that the same method was not going to work here. Simply putting in extra hours at the office was not enough; you needed to network outside office hours too.

The first time she had accepted an invite she had stood out like a sore thumb in her office gear, but now she'd become something of an expert at making a seamless transition from day to evening and had it down to an impressive five minutes in the ladies' room to make the necessary adjustments.

Like anything in life, it was about organisation: first make-up refreshed, lips highlighted for the evening by a bold red lipstick, then her hair, released from the sleek ponytail secured at the nape of her neck; one quick shake and it fell in glossy waves down her narrow back.

All achieved while she was exchanging the discreet studs in her ears for a pair of art deco jet chandelier drops.

The tailored jacket that had seen her through the day's meetings was removed and the stark simplicity of the little black dress it had covered was jazzed up with an oversized art deco pendant tonight. The jacket, neatly folded, was inside her capacious designer bag along with the moderate heels she had swapped for a pair of spiky ankle boots; that part took two minutes, tops.

It was amazing what you could do when you were organised and Gwen was incredibly focused. That was how she had made it this far. She didn't allow herself to be distracted; she knew what she wanted and then figured out the quickest way to achieve her goal. People had quickly started to notice. She'd overheard a conversation in the ladies' room once, and she had wondered, curiously, who this *ruthless* person was that they were discussing.

Then she'd found out it was her.

'You're just jealous, Trish, that Gwen has got the face and body to sleep her way to the top,' had been one of the cruel comments she'd overheard.

Crossing one slim, shapely ankle over the other, she turned her head and laughed because everyone else was. The anger she had felt that day in the Ladies was spent now, but the memory still had the power to make the tension climb into her shoulders. She put her hand on the back of her neck and rotated her head from side to side to ease it.

In one aspect they had been right—she *was* determined to succeed—but the totally unfair implication that she ever would demean herself by sleeping her way to the top… It had hurt and made her want to rush out and challenge the women cattily bitching about her, but just as well the tears streaming down her face had made her reject this impulse, because it was far better to make them eat their words by simply being better than them, and proving herself.

Blurting out that actually she was a virgin would not have improved the situation; it was almost easier all round to be considered an ambitious slut with no morals.

'You look fierce!' Louise, who had been the

new girl in the corporate finance department before Gwen had arrived, looked at her with raised eyebrows. 'Do you want another drink?'

Gwen shook her head and smiled as she held her hand over her full glass. She turned and caught sight of herself in the mirror that lined the wall behind the bar. Her loose hair had a mirror gloss, but the cost, which had initially seemed enormous, of having her thick chestnut waves tamed by the hand of someone who was a superstar in the world of hairdressing had proved to be a good investment, she decided, taking a sip of her wine. She intended to make it last all evening—the buzz of being here in this city was all the stimulation she needed.

Gwen leaned in to catch what the woman beside Louise was saying.

'Your Scots accent is just so cute, everyone thinks so.'

*When they're not thinking I'm sleeping my way to the top,* Gwen thought, hiding her flash of bitterness behind a smile. As she had to virtually yell to make herself heard above the competing conversations, Gwen decided it required less effort to smile and nod rather than correct the woman's mistake over her nationality, even though it felt as though she was betraying her Welsh roots.

Not that anyone back home would have recognised her—the once awkward, intense swot with the glasses—in this place, she thought wryly, leaning in again to catch what Louise was saying.

'Don't look now but *he* hasn't taken his eyes off you since he came in.' Louise's eyes widened as she tipped her head towards the smoky glass wall that screened the bar from the street. 'I said don't look!'

'I wasn't going to.' Gwen was not averse to the idea of romance, at the right time, but it wasn't scheduled at this point in her life. Right now it came under the heading of a distraction she didn't need. Still it was always good if someone appreciated the effort she had made with her appearance.

Louise took a sip of her cocktail and sighed, leaning sideways to look over Gwen's shoulder. 'He really is totally…oh, my God!' she yelped, before hissing, 'He's coming over, don't panic.'

Gwen heard his voice before she saw him,

deep, with a light gravel underlying the velvet and an intriguing hint of an accent. It made the half-smile she was wearing in response to her friend's antics quiver and fade as for some inexplicable reason a deep shiver that made her toes curl passed through her body.

It was that same voice that dragged Gwen away now from the New York bar and the exact moment when her five-year plan—*My God, was I really that arrogant, or was I just incredibly young and naive?*—had started falling apart. She was back to sitting in the school's assembly hall where for some inexplicable reason Rio Bardales, billionaire heir to the Bardales empire, was holding his audience in the palm of his strong brown elegant hand. Gwen had a sudden unwelcome image of that hand, those tapering fingers sliding over pale skin...her skin... She gulped and blinked to clear the unwanted images dancing in her head.

Everyone was clapping, except Gwen. She couldn't have, even if she had wanted to. What she actually wanted, what every cell in her body was screaming at her to do, was to run as far away as she could.

Her head turned fractionally from side to side in mute denial—*this cannot be happening!*

'He looks like a film star.' Ruth's awed whisper brought the past back with a rush she had no defence against. She remembered thinking exactly the same thing that night in the stylish New York bar where they'd met. He'd been wearing a suit then too but it had looked as though he might have slept in it, yet he'd still looked absolutely gorgeous—how could he not? Even if you discounted his physical attributes—several inches over six feet tall; long-limbed without being in any way lanky; lean and muscular with broad shoulders and a natural athletic elegance—Rio's strong-boned symmetrical features were arresting enough to be a conversation-stopper. His eyes, dark and almond-shaped, were almost black, framed by dense long lashes and set beneath strongly defined flyaway brows, his carved cheekbones sharp enough to cut, and his square chin had the hint of a cleft, but it was his beautifully cut, overtly sensual mouth that did the most damage to her nervous system.

Gwen felt dizzy as the image from the past was overlaid by one of the man standing on the stage, his words just sounds that had a physical effect on her, sending successive shivers over the surface of her suddenly too warm skin.

She felt as though everyone *must* see what was happening, that they were all staring at her, but crazily they were completely oblivious. Now they were laughing, an appreciative ripple of sound that wafted like a breeze through the vaulted room—Rio was being amusing, entertaining. She knew full well, though, that he could get a *lot* more entertaining than this, especially when there was skin-to-skin contact involved.

Jaw clenched, lips compressed over the cry trying to escape her lips, she closed her eyes and thought, *Do not go there, Gwen...* But too late—she was already remembering that first shock of feeling skin-to-skin contact after he had unfastened her bra for the first time and, holding her eyes, had pulled her hard against his chest...

* * *

The myriad impressions made her dizzy: the warmth of his skin, the clean salty tang she'd breathed in, the tingling of intense pleasure as her hardened nipples pressed into the barrier of his naked, muscled chest.

His eyes didn't leave hers for one moment, the hot desire burning in them making her limbs go boneless, silencing the voice telling her she needed to explain to him that she didn't have a clue what she was doing. It had seemed a matter of simple politeness only a few minutes ago, but now she found herself thinking in a hazy way what did it actually matter…?

Why shouldn't her embarrassing inexperience remain on a need-to-know basis? After all, he'd not twigged yet so why should it matter? She could suddenly see all the advantages of sleeping with a stranger: you didn't owe them anything, including explanations… Ironic, really, when this was precisely what *he* pointed out to her a few days later in a frigid voice filled with icy contempt she would never, ever forget…even though she had tried.

'I owe you nothing, certainly not explanations. We had sex; we are not in a relationship.'

The brutal words carried the impact of a sledgehammer, each individual scornful syllable adding fresh layers of hurt as she clutched his shirt around her. Unable to match his marvellous unselfconscious attitude to nudity, she had pulled it on to walk to the bathroom, and it retained the scent of his skin but it didn't give her a warm feeling of intimacy; she felt mortified and stupid and very, *very* cold.

She lifted her chin, struggling to salvage a tiny shred of pride. 'I... I didn't think we were.' It wasn't totally a lie; she knew that a few nights of passion did not add up to a relationship. It nearly hadn't even made it this far after he'd found out he was her first lover and hadn't exactly been thrilled about it, and he'd been quite clear then that this was not the start of anything; it was just casual fun he was offering.

Pride and the determination not to give him the satisfaction of knowing that she had just begun to believe that they'd developed a deeper connection made her stand her ground rather than run away. She felt stupid even imagining for a moment that when he'd told her she was the best sex he'd ever had, it meant he thought she was different and what they had was worth more than a quick fling. It was easy to see *now* that it had all been wishful thinking on her part.

Maybe he'd known anyway because in case she'd missed the point he drove it home with brutal honesty.

'We are not exclusive, you and I. You do not have the right to interrogate me.'

The chill in his eyes, the hauteur in his body language, the expressive curl of his lip did not require the addition of the snap of his fingers to tell her she was being dismissed, not just from his bed or this room, but from his life.

'Who I sleep with…and, let me tell you, it is never *knowingly* anyone who would rifle through my private correspondence…is none of your concern.'

She tried to defend herself, tell him that wasn't what she'd been doing, she really did, but she failed. Basically, because the bottom line was that it was true she *had* read his letter, but not intentionally. She'd picked up the incriminating piece of paper off the floor along with the pile of other correspondence that had landed on the carpet when she had caught it with her elbow. She was unable to replicate the precision of the neat stack but, tongue caught between her teeth, she had been making an effort to do so when the letterhead had caught her eye. She had scanned a sentence before she had realised what she was doing and…she really s*hould* have stopped; that was why she knew the guilt had been shining in her eyes when he'd caught her in the act.

She had considered pretending she hadn't read it, but it would have looked foolish.

As it turned out that wasn't even an option as the awkward words just blurted out of her mouth in the face of his accusatory glare.

'I only said, "So you have a child…" I didn't know, that's all. Are you and the mother together?' She felt the blood drain from her face. 'You're not…not married, are you?'

He arched a brow. 'Would it have mattered to you if I were?'

She wanted to slap him then, and she had never struck anyone in her life, she couldn't even crush a spider, but it took all her control to keep her clenched hand at her side, refusing to rise to the insulting provocation.

'What is his name?' There was no reason he shouldn't have a child, several children, in fact, and no reason either that he should have mentioned it to her…because he had made it quite clear that what they were enjoying had a shelf life. She was the one who had decided something had changed—and now it had.

He was the sort of man whose response to the news that he was a father was to demand a DNA test; he was the sort of man who, when asked his son's name by her, replied that he couldn't remember! The irony was that she'd learnt more in the last twenty seconds about this man than she had in three whole days… or, rather, nights.

He arched a dark brow and regarded her with frozen distaste. She had caught glimpses of the hauteur before but had never been on the blighting, chilly receiving end of it.

'What business is it of yours if I have a child?' His voice carried no expression but it didn't need to as his eyes said it all.

'None at all,' she agreed as the paper in her fingers that outlined in black and white a DNA match fluttered to the floor. 'So it confirms you're a father, so what? It takes more than a piece of paper to become one of those, doesn't it? Paternity has very little to do with being a father—that's all about a lifetime commitment, not just donating your genes—so I really hope this kid has someone else in his life who doesn't need proof that they're related to him, and someone who actually remembers his name.'

With a sneer of contempt that was aimed as much at herself as at him, she gathered her dignity around her as she removed his shirt and, with a grimace of distaste, she dropped it on the floor before she walked away with her head held high.

# CHAPTER TWO

RIO WAITED FOR a polite ripple of laughter to die down before he moved on. His mother, who he was standing in for, could do this sort of thing in her sleep and she'd been genuinely upset that she couldn't attend today, which proved, he supposed, that there were some people who enjoyed their schooldays and wanted to be reminded of them. His glance slid over the young shiny faces turned to him.

Were there any lonely kids out there who cried themselves to sleep when the lights went out? Not that he'd been traumatised by being sent off at a ridiculously young age to an English boarding school, just stifled, perhaps.

The fact that he and his twin brother, Roman, were each other's support group meant he'd never suffered the sort of isolation that had afflicted some of the other children, and there had been enough foreign students at his school to make his own accent nothing to set him apart. Despite the fact he had survived the experience relatively unscathed, sending his children to boarding school was a tradition that he intended to break, not because he was rebelling against tradition, but because he didn't intend to have children at all.

He felt the phone in his pocket vibrate and resisted the temptation to cut the obligatory amusing anecdote short. Nothing in his delivery would make his audience suspect he had moved onto autopilot and was working out how soon he would be able to make his exit. Instead of his speech, his thoughts were on the rescue package he was putting into place for a friend. Jake was so grateful to him, which made him feel guilty. It hadn't required much effort on his part to save Jake—the name Bardales inspired confidence and made those banks who didn't appreciate that his friend was a techno genius a lot more likely to extend credit.

'Again, thank you, Mr Jarvis, for asking me here to present the Cavendish Prize in my mother's stead.' Rio turned to look at the headmaster before he could launch into another speech. 'My mother sends her apologies for being unable to be present herself today, as this school still holds such a special place in her heart. However, she is here in spirit and I believe her presence is still marked on several desks where she left a permanent impression. So without further ado...' He took the crystal cup from the female teacher who held it out. 'I present this award to this year's recipient of the Cavendish Prize, Clarice Walker.'

Smiling, he watched a tall girl who was blushing as brightly as her auburn curls walk from the back of the room towards the stage, her progress accompanied by clapping.

He handed the girl the crystal goblet engraved with her name and the envelope that contained a more practical reward in the form of a cheque.

'Congratulations, Clarice. My mother is looking forward to meeting you in the near future when she is more mobile.'

In the meantime, his normally very active parent was being a predictably pretty impatient patient, frustrated by the plaster cast that was her souvenir from a recent skiing trip.

He took a step back and joined in the clapping as the youngster took her place in front of the microphone. 'Thank you, Mr Bardales. I do hope your mother is better very soon.'

His mother was fond of saying that being involved with young people kept her young, but being in this room filled with shiny idealism and even shinier faces made him feel old and not a little nostalgic for a touch of youthful rebellion—if there were any mavericks in the room, they were hiding it well.

It was hard to disguise his inner cynicism as he scanned the sea of faces staring up at the stage listening to the earnest speaker, wondering how long it would be before the real world would kill off all this youthful enthusiasm.

His thought stream was interrupted when the room suddenly erupted into sniggers at what he could only assume was an 'in joke' from Clarice. Rio fought an eye-roll, recognising with a jolt that he was displaying all the characteristics of a grumpy old man at only thirty-one—it did not bode well for the future.

Rio let his eyelids droop, the silky mesh of his lashes hiding the gleam of cynicism shining in the dark depths. *Perhaps,* he mused, *I need a day off...* Or a night in with someone smart and beautiful who had no interest in what made him tick, but just wanted to use this body that was actually in better condition than he deserved, considering the schedule that had left very little time for the punishing exercise regime he had once enjoyed.

His mobile mouth curled into a smile that flattened out as a movement in the periphery of his vision interrupted the pleasant fantasy before he had even begun to weave it, dragging his wandering attention to the rows of children sitting nearest the stage.

*Finally* a bit of rebellion! He didn't fight off his grin as he watched one of the tiny occupants of the low bench just in front of the stage making a determined bid for freedom.

Rio silently willed him on, but inevitably he didn't get far. The culprit was captured by someone who displayed a great deal of agility and also a really good bottom…actually, it was truly excellent, he decided, studying the curves outlined by conservative trousers that were wide-legged but pulled tight across her bottom as she stretched. The tall, leggy owner of the rich chestnut hair and excellent bottom released her hold on the kid's arm, bending a little lower to say something that involved a wag of her finger, and, although he dragged his feet, the sulky little boy retook his seat.

He was attempting to pull his attention back to the proceedings on stage when the woman straightened up, one hand smoothing her glorious hair, the other smoothing the fabric of her trousers over long thighs. He was on the point of looking away when she lifted her head and they made eye contact.

The connection lasted seconds before she turned away, head bent to the child, but it only took a fraction of that time for his self-possession to fragment into a million pieces as recognition shuddered through him with the force of a sledgehammer blow that continued to send aftershocks throughout his body. He lowered his eyelids to shield his eyes as he nodded, mainly because everyone else was doing it in response to something the headmaster was saying.

Confusion was not normally part of Rio's mindset, as confusion required an uncertainty, a hesitancy, an inability to cut through all the nonsense. None of these were attitudes he possessed, and he was rarely confused, but as he stood there questioning the evidence of his own eyes Rio was extremely confused.

It was the sort of confusion that came from seeing a familiar face out of context. Rio struggled to kick start his brain and think past the sense-limiting testosterone rush.

What the hell was this high-flyer doing in a school for kids of moneyed parents, wearing an outfit that made it easy for her to bend over and grab the would-be escapee kid—wide-legged trousers cinched in with a belt at her slender waist and a shirt that might have been sexy had it not been buttoned up to the neck?

If he ever thought about Welsh Gwen, he pictured her in a New York setting, dressed with immaculate City gloss, in sharp-edged fashionable tailoring that made sure people took her seriously despite the extraordinary face that was always going to set her apart from the other ambitious women aiming to shatter any glass ceilings that got in their way. And good luck to them; he liked ambitious women, just not ones who thought they could control him.

*If* he ever thought about her…? *Who are you*

*kidding, Rio?* he mocked himself as he fought to regain control of his stupefied brain. The dressed part was a lie too; he always pictured her completely naked and lying beneath him, her stunning legs wrapped tightly around him.

It had been nearly three years since he'd last seen her, and, despite the fact he was not someone to dwell on past mistakes, his subconscious had been known to drag him back to this particularly gorgeous mistake time and time again.

His eyes slid over her rear; he was thinking of the sleek curves under the clothes and an image flashed into his head of the last time he had seen her, walking away from him stark naked, anger and pride in her slow determined strides. He remembered every detail: her lovely long legs, her slender square shoulders, the graceful curve of her spine and feminine flare of her hips from a tiny waist. Thinking about the dimple just above her taut right buttock and the endless graceful legs sent a fresh flash of hormonal heat through his body.

He had spent considerable time and effort rationalising how their short liaison had left such a lasting raw impression on him, convincing himself that it was the element of unfinished business between them, thanks to that messy conclusion. All wasted energy as it turned out, as in reality he was unable to file the episode away in some dusty mental drawer marked 'Over' because he had never known a woman who had made him this *hungry*!

Though in his defence Gwen Meredith, with her melodic lilting voice, was not a woman a man forgot. *Any* man with blood in his veins could not be indifferent to the memory of the electricity that had been between them, the little whimpered purr low in her throat whenever he'd slid his tongue between her plump lips… He inhaled sharply. *Dios*, this raw hunger was something he had not experienced before or since her; in fact, the memory had made any encounters he'd had since Gwen seem pallid and boring in comparison. He frowned and pushed away the sense-paralysing fantasies before they took hold, focusing instead on the mystery of her presence—here, where there were no glass ceilings whatsoever to shatter.

How and why the hell had she transplanted

herself from New York to the English shires and a private school in leafy grounds?

He'd always enjoyed the challenge of unravelling a mystery.

It wasn't until Max tried to twist out of her grip that Gwen realised she still had hold of his hand.

'Sit down, Max.'

Her voice was lacking its usual note of calm authority and sounded as though it were coming from a long way off. The fact the child had ignored her did not at that moment feel like something that Gwen could deal with, when standing up was taking all her focus, and her head was still spinning.

She pressed her hand to her stomach, and squeezed her eyes shut. She couldn't excuse the liquid heat of desire in the pit of her belly on ignorance, she was simply stupid and weak and...

*Oh, stop bleating, Gwen, and deal with it!*

A tiny sigh huffed between her clenched lips as her slender shoulders lowered and her chin lifted fractionally in response to the bracing inner voice that had zero tolerance for self-pity.

It was one thing to acknowledge you had a problem, it was another entirely to find yourself staring it straight in the face. It left little room to hide from the fact, mortifying and shameful but inescapable, that when it came to Rio her hormones were utterly indiscriminate, though in her defence there couldn't be many men who projected the aura of raw sexuality that he did.

She wasted one wistful moment wishing for a time when she had sincerely believed that respect and liking were necessary for sexual attraction, when she had believed that being paralysed with lust by an obsidian-eyed stare had anything to do with a mystical connection. No, actually she wasn't wistful at all; it was scary to think how beneath her sophisticated facade she had been so totally vulnerable. She had had nearly three years to think about it and she had come to the conclusion that it had all been about her belated sexual awakening allied with her inexperience and timing. Yes, most importantly, it was always about the timing.

She'd told herself it could have been anyone who had sparked her desire; it had just happened to be Rio Bardales who had provided the catalyst, and the idea he wasn't special whatsoever had been oddly comforting.

Misplaced comfort, as it happened. The second she'd seen him again she'd felt sick to her stomach and scared stiff. He had recognised her too—she had seen it in his eyes. The question was would he be curious enough to seek her out, talk to her, try and find out why she was here instead of New York? She clamped her lips tight over a snort of self-disgust for the idiot she had been. The simple fact was, she might have known a whole lot about financial forecasting, but when it came to life and men she just hadn't had a clue.

Maybe she was paranoid after all, thinking he'd recognised her? She bore little resemblance to the sophisticated career girl on the fast track to success, with her designer clothes and strong sense of self-belief that she could achieve whatever she set her mind to.

Right now her mind was set to getting the hell out of here, as soon as humanly possible.

'Max needs the bathroom,' she hissed in Ruth's ear.

Ruth started to get to her feet but responded to the pressure of Gwen's hand on her shoulder and subsided back down.

'I don't want—'

Gwen smiled determinedly at the little boy. 'Yes, you do…'

Looking slightly bewildered but not at all unwilling to leave the boring assembly, he trotted along beside Gwen as she made her dash for the side door.

Once in the cool, emotional calm of the long corridor lined with photographs of sporting achievements down the years of pupils past and present, she realised that she had really not handled that very well at all. In fact, probably the only thing she'd achieved was to draw attention to herself.

'Miss…?'

'Oh, yes, right.' Her heels tapping on the floor, she led the boy to the nearest cloakroom.

'Off you go. I'll be waiting.'

Her excuse for escape vanished inside the boys' cloakroom and Gwen let out a sigh as she leaned back against the wall.

*This isn't the time to panic*, she told herself.
*If not now, when?*

She ignored the unhelpful insertion of her subconscious and reminded herself that Ellie was safely in the crèche, where it was most unlikely their VIP would be taken—the red-brick addition to the listed building was only a selling point to members of staff. No, he'd be taking the well-trodden route beginning in the photo gallery of alumni who had gone on to success and fame or, in some cases, had just had it handed to them on a plate, taking in the new state-of-the-art science block and then heading back via the restored, historically listed gardens for refreshments in the head-master's office.

She was safe and so, more importantly, was Ellie.

But she didn't dare relax; people didn't when nightmares started happening for real. Hand to her mouth, she straightened up and began to pace up and down until the trembling weakness in her legs made her stop. She placed her hands on the window sill, staring out at the quadrangle with its borders of herbs she had supervised her class planting last week.

It *was* going to be fine but she had to pre-pare for the worst, and hope…*really* hope for the best. Her smooth brow furrowed. The most important question was, how bad could the worst be?

This was a situation she had never antici-pated happening when she had made her deci-sion not to make contact with him after she'd discovered she was pregnant. It hadn't been an easy choice to make or one she had ever foreseen she would have to. Having children had been something she had seen for herself, but only in the distant future when she was in a secure, loving relationship and had got far enough up the career ladder to be able to af-ford to step off the escalator temporarily and then afford excellent child care afterwards.

She was very conscious of the argument that morally a man had a right to know when he'd fathered a child and a child had a right to know who her father was, but what if that father had no interest in being a father? He'd demanded DNA proof of paternity once, she thought scornfully, so why would this time have been any different?

During her pregnancy there had been moments when she knew she wouldn't ever tell him and others when she had come so close to making contact. She'd even composed emails she'd never sent. They'd generally been along the lines of I thought you should know, but don't worry, it's fine that you're not going to be involved in our child's life, but any relevant family medical history would be appreciated.

She had see-sawed back and forth as she wrestled with the difficult choice throughout her pregnancy. There had been a deep sense of relief when she had finally made her decision while looking down with a sense of wonderment at her perfect newborn daughter, experiencing a swell of protective love she had never realised existed until that moment.

Why was she worrying about the rights of an accidental father who thought parenthood was just about making a genetic contribution? Presumably he'd ask her for DNA proof too. How could a man like that, a reluctant father, be good for her daughter? After all, this was all about what was best for her baby. Holding the warm, perfect person she had given life to, the cold-bloodedness of Rio's attitude to being a father chilled her. She decided then and there that this baby would never know she had a father who didn't want her.

After all, Gwen knew exactly what that felt like. She might have no siblings but growing up she hadn't been the only child in the house. Her father was a man who expected to be the centre of attention at all times. Gwen had learnt not to compete with him for her mother's attention, but it hadn't stopped him resenting her existence.

She didn't know how old she had been, or even how she had found out that her serial-adulterer father had had his first affair when her mother had been pregnant with her. In his eyes that, at least, was an excuse for his behaviour. After that it seemed things had gone downhill, although to the outside world they had continued to present the image of a happy, perfect family—and it had all started with the birth of the baby he'd never wanted anyway.

And now Gwen's decision not to tell Rio he was a father, which had seemed so right at the time, was being severely tested. She had made it assuming that their lives would never intersect again. Because what were the odds? They lived in totally different worlds. She remembered the day she had seen a missed call on her phone and recognised his number. It had been a very weak moment and if she'd picked up she might, just might, have told him. Though imagining his face if he had seen her the way she was that day, attached to a drip in a hospital ward unable to keep any fluids down, made her very glad she hadn't. She hadn't felt lucky at the time but now she knew that some women suffered that sort of debilitating nausea all through their pregnancy. For her it had only lasted five months, which had been more than long enough.

'Miss… Miss…'

Gwen shook her head and turned to the little boy standing there. He'd washed his face a little too enthusiastically and his hair was wet, as was the front of his uniform shirt. She felt a tug of affection and smiled. She had fallen into teaching through a mixture of accidents and necessity, but she loved it.

'What have you got there?' she asked, looking at his cupped chubby hands.

'A bee, a big, big bee! It was stuck on the window.' He lifted his hands to his ear. 'It's still buzzing but he won't sting me. He's a nice bee.'

Gwen sincerely hoped this *nice* bee lived up to expectations and hastily opened the window, letting in a waft of warm scented summer air and the murmur of young voices as pupils began to file out of the hall and through the wide stone arch at the far end of the quadrangle. She picked up her damp pupil and she smiled encouragingly until he opened his hand, giving his captive freedom.

'Ah, there she is now.'

Gwen's smile became fixed as she froze, only the child in her arms preventing her from humiliating herself by ducking down out of sight. The headmaster didn't appear to notice her deer-in-headlights pose, framed in the window as he looked at the man standing beside him.

'Mrs Meredith, I was just telling Mr Bardales...'

'Rio, please—'

The headmaster tipped his head in pleased acknowledgement. 'How *interested* his mother was when I was telling her of your enthusiasm for outdoor teaching.'

'I share her enthusiasm,' Rio lied without a flicker and bared his white teeth in a smile that did not touch his eyes as they drifted down her body, or what he could see of it.

Self-preservation kept her expression blank as the shock, guilt and fear that paralysed her were virtually obliterated beneath a shameful hot thrum of sexual awareness that made her legs tremble. Her nerve endings were screaming out in recognition as she turned away from the window and, after taking a deep soothing breath, opened the adjacent door and stepped outside.

The headmaster beamed, blissfully oblivious of any undercurrents seething around him. 'Excellent...well, we have the expert here to explain.' He gave an impatient little shake of his head. 'Come along, Mrs Meredith.' He paused and lifted a hand. 'Ah, here is your class now.'

She huffed out a sigh of relief, saved by the bell—or at least by the scuffle of twenty pairs of small feet as the reception class, with Ruth bringing up the rear, came filing out of the hall into the archway.

All she had to do now was to walk past Rio

and she was home free. She clenched her jaw and with determined optimism told herself that this could still turn out all right.

'There you go.' She put down the child still in her arms, took his hand and led him towards the arch, where, the moment he saw his classmates, he took off, ignoring the headmaster's bellow of 'No running!' as he pounded across the gravel to join his friends, the tiny stones scattering in his enthusiasm.

It was an enthusiasm to get away that Gwen shared.

Careful not to make eye contact with Rio, her heart pumping frantically beneath her pale blue cotton blouse as she struggled to channel calm indifference, she nodded towards the head and made to join her class.

'No, Mrs Meredith.'

She stopped and sighed, her eyes following her class as she thought wistfully, *So near and yet so far,* before squaring her shoulders and turning back, an expression of polite enquiry painted on her face.

'Come and explain to our guest about your initiative. I admit I had my doubts initially but I have been won over,' he said graciously.

'We have even included it in our new prospec-
tus and the parents are most enthusiastic…
but now I'll allow our expert to explain,' he
added to Rio as Gwen joined them, struggling
to hide her reluctance. 'I will leave you in her
very capable hands.'

'My class—' Gwen protested, clutching at
straws.

'If you could bring our guest to my office at
two-thirty, the governors are joining us there
for coffee.'

'I shall look forward to that,' Rio, who up
to this point had been fully intending to find
himself regretfully having to leave long before
any convivial chat over coffee, assured with
plausible sincerity.

Gwen pulled in a breath and, thinking it was
now or never, forced herself to meet his stare
head-on. She had chosen to forget about the
skin-tingling effect of his proximity, because,
until you were actually feeling it, the aura of
raw masculinity he exuded was hard to quan-
tify.

She struggled to think past it and waited.

His expression was one of unstudied cool,
a calmness contradicted by his hands, which

were clenched into fists at his side. 'So, *Mrs* Meredith, this is a surprise.'

'Yes,' she agreed, relieved and slightly amazed that she sounded so calm. Now all she had to do was string two words together in the right order and make an excuse to leave, after finding someone else to dump him on. That shouldn't be too difficult, as she was certain she wasn't the only female who couldn't see past the packaging.

She allowed her eyes to sweep up scornfully from his toes to his face, but midway through their journey the scorn got lost. All right, in her defence, it was *very* pretty packaging.

# CHAPTER THREE

'SO, YOU'RE MARRIED?' She had not adopted her husband's surname, but that was not unusual these days. The thought that she was married lay in a tight knot in his belly, his own reaction surprising him. Or maybe like his own mother she was divorced and now went by her maiden name?

A speculative crease appeared in his brow as she looked at him like a cornered animal and said nothing...which suggested that perhaps things were not all smooth sailing on the marriage front.

'Does your husband work at the school too?' he asked, instinctively disliking with a vengeance this unknown sexist jerk who had asked her to give up her dreams for him, leave her high-flying career and bury herself here... in sensible clothes.

His nostrils flared in outraged contempt as his glance slid to the flare of her hips below the cinched-in waist. The undeniable fact was she would look desirable in a sack. He didn't probe too deeply into the question of *why* the idea of her falling in love with some guy deeply enough to give up everything she'd worked so hard for made him so angry, then decided that it was the waste of talent. It was her choice, obviously, but she'd probably end up resenting the man at some point in future.

*You didn't want her but you don't want anyone else to have her*, suggested the sly voice in his head.

'It's been lovely to catch up,' she said brightly.

He laughed. 'Is that the conversational version of fake news?'

Gwen's polite mask slipped. What did he want her to say?

The truth was a luxury she didn't have, which narrowed her conversational options. Veiling the animosity she knew he had to be seeing in her eyes, she lowered her lashes to half mast and continued doggedly as though she hadn't heard his sarcastic insertion.

'But I really should get back to my class. They'll be running riot, and—'

'I thought you were going to explain to me about your outdoor teaching scheme.'

'Because you're *so* interested.' And she was so in trouble, if the head overheard her talking to the guest of honour that way. She saw the flare of interest in the glitter of his dark-framed eyes...the lush eyelashes his daughter had inherited...and wished the words unsaid.

'Absolutely,' he came back, not missing a beat.

She tightened her lips and this time didn't react to the provocation. 'Fine.'

'Outdoor learning sounds a bit New Age and *out there* for a place like this.' His eyes swept across the black and white Tudor building behind her.

His sneering attitude really riled her, despite the fact she knew full well that his interest was feigned. She could only assume he was enjoying making her feel uncomfortable. She snorted. As if *he* weren't born to a life of privilege.

'Because you went to an inner-city school, of course.' The words popped out before she could stop them. Flustered, she slid her eyes from his, her cheeks burning with embarrassment that she'd lost her cool.

'Did you?'

Surprise brought her eyes back to his. Dizzied by the direct eye-to-eye connection, she brought her lashes down in a protective shield that cast shadows across the curve of her high, smooth cheekbones. She gave her head the tiniest of shakes.

'No, I was brought up in a smallish market town in mid Wales.'

The primary school had been overcrowded after several large estates had mushroomed around the town. After that, she had taken the bus with everyone else to the red-brick comprehensive in the nearest large town.

He had asked the question, she had answered, and he felt…?

What?

They had been as intimate as two people could be, he had explored every inch of her body and she had shown an endless fascination for his, and yet, other than conversations that involved work, he knew virtually nothing about her. But then this shouldn't be so surprising; intimacy outside the bedroom was not something Rio did.

It was a choice, and he didn't feel as though he was missing out on anything. If there were occasions in the cooling aftermath of satisfying sex that made him conscious of a nebulous feeling of something that could be called emptiness, he considered it a price worth paying to avoid drifting into a relationship where he'd be expected to profess feelings he didn't believe existed, or, even worse, might convince himself *did*. His own father had never stopped believing he loved someone, even when it had nearly destroyed the person he'd claimed to love.

She saw a flicker of awareness move across the dark surface of his eyes before he lowered his gaze, frustrating her curiosity.

And why was she acting as if that were a *bad* thing? Gwen told herself she didn't want to know what made this man tick. She wanted him and his disruptive aura the hell out of her life.

'So tell me about outdoor teaching.'

Her shoulders lifted in a fractional shrug and she began by hoping to bore him but then, despite herself, warming to the subject until she heard herself talking about key-stage attainment and came to an abrupt halt. There was boring and then there was being an anorak.

'So you're basically telling me that kids are more engaged when learning outdoors?'

It wasn't as if she hadn't come across the sceptical response before, and was usually tolerant of it, but in this instance her chin came up. 'Quite definitely,' she said confidently. 'Learning through direct experience gives a greater understanding and research shows it raises academic attainment and—'

'It's fun,' he cut in with a quirky smile that made her heart flip. He thrust one hand in the pocket of his trousers and pulled out a vibrating phone. Silencing the low purr, he replaced it without even glancing at the screen. 'Relax.'

Gwen almost laughed at the advice, and so would he if he knew about Ellie. No, he probably wouldn't be laughing at all, but what he would be doing remained something of a question mark, and she was quite happy for it to remain that way.

'I'm all for anything that doesn't involve falling asleep in a stuffy classroom, although it might be tough to do in a city. But here—' his glance took in the parkland that surrounded the school buildings '—you have the advantage in that you don't have to go far to find a green space.'

'It's very lovely,' she agreed gravely. Who would have known when she got up this morning that in just a few short hours she'd be discussing the countryside with the father of her child? How long would it be before they got onto the topic of the weather?

'But not a cheap place to set up home?' he asked, clearly digging for information on what job her so-called husband did.

'We live in a cottage in the grounds.' Now, if he chose to assume that the *we* she referred to was a husband, that was his business. She hadn't lied; not that she wouldn't if she had to in order to protect Ellie. The problem was she wasn't very good at it. For once she was thoroughly glad of the outdated tradition in the school—so far unchallenged—which meant that every female teacher, regardless of her marital status, was referred to as *Mrs*.

The muscles along Rio's jaw clenched and he had a sour taste in his mouth as her words conjured an image of bucolic domesticity. He had never craved for domesticity, bucolic or otherwise.

Being bound to your soul mate for life might be some people's dream, but it definitely wasn't his. Leaving aside the fact that soul mates occupied the same space in his brain as unicorns, to him the marriage contract was not a cause for celebration and certainly not one he ever planned to put his name to.

He was ready to concede that it was possible not *all* marriages were toxic—perhaps even his parents' marriage had had a honeymoon period—but why take the chance? He'd often been called a risk-taker in business, but his risks were calculated and based more on facts than speculation. Marriage was just a risk too far for him.

The sound of a child crying behind him provided a distracting respite from his thoughts, but, respite or not, the wail had a nerve-shredding intensity and brought an expression of pained irritation to his face. However, the irritation turned to speculation when he saw the expression on Gwen's face. She was frozen with fear, but this was the first time he had seen it. The only movement was provided by her long lashes fluttering like some exotic butterfly's wings against her bone-white skin and the rapid rise and fall of her breasts under the blue cotton shirt that looked like a paler version of her striking cobalt eyes. She looked so dreadful he was convinced she was about to pass out and he tensed, ready to catch her before she hit the ground.

Then, as he watched, she unfroze like a statue coming to slow life, her eyes swivelling from a point beyond his shoulder to his face. A tiny amount of colour seeped back into her skin, robbing it of its marble appearance, and her expression was now almost...*resigned*? The furrow between his darkly etched straight brows deepened, but before he could ask what was wrong an older woman dressed in a floral-print dress that looked as if she'd fashioned it out of the curtains of a small bungalow rushed past, barging him with her elbow as she struggled to soothe the child she was carrying. He was no expert but this tiny dark-haired bundle did not look anywhere near school age, although she did look as though she might be rather a handful.

'Gwen, I'm so sorry,' the crèche assistant gasped. 'We simply couldn't pacify her; she just wants you, I'm afraid.'

'Has she been like this for—?'

'No, it's only been the last half-hour.'

'Don't worry, that's fine.' Gwen held out her arms, and Ellie, still sobbing, wrapped her arms and legs limpet-wise around her. Hot and sticky, the heat of her small body penetrated through Gwen's shirt and made her think of that first moment when Ellie had been laid on her chest, so warm and heavy. 'Hush, sweetheart, I know…' She smiled at the other woman feeling oddly calm now the worst was actually happening and she had no other option than to just deal with it. 'Thanks and don't worry.'

'Poor sweetheart…' The motherly woman stroked the child's dark hair before turning away. 'I have to get back, Gwen.'

'Of course and thanks again. I had a feeling she wasn't right this morning and I wish I'd kept her home now.' She had time owing in lieu of the sixth-form economics after-school club she had filled in for last month. It was a role she'd originally arrived at the school to take up, covering maternity leave. She'd had nothing to go to afterwards and the offer of a six-month stint in the reception class had seemed like a gift.

At the end of the six months she had been offered a permanent contract and she had found her niche in a place it would never have occurred to her to look. The days when she imagined that monetary rewards and kudos would make her happy seemed a long time ago.

Rio found himself rooted to the spot as the cogs in his brain clicked incredibly slowly. He considered the facts in front of him, but, despite a reality that was literally staring him in the face, it still took him a few seconds for comprehension to dawn. He waited until the pretty floral woman moved outside hearing distance before he spoke.

'She's yours.' He ignored the twisting sensation in his chest; the problem was all in his head, where Gwen had remained frozen in time as the incredibly desirable, ambitious young executive who had seemed so sweet, so open and honest, that he'd started to feel guilty, among other things, that their affair was only temporary, until he'd caught her reading his correspondence. It had instantly resurrected toxic memories of watching his father read his mother's mail, take her phone and check her messages, delete numbers *he* felt she didn't need. *Dios*, he'd only just got his head around Gwen being married and now it seemed she was a mother too.

'Yes…now, if you'll excuse us…'

'Hold on!' He bent down.

She ran her tongue across her dry lips and tightened her grip on the child, who now lay limp in her arms. It looked as if the crying had tired her out; she was almost asleep.

Rio straightened up and held out the dog-eared stuffed rabbit that the little girl had dropped.

'Is this yours?'

He waited as the child's head lifted from her mother's shoulder. She regarded him with deep suspicious eyes like velvety brown pansies before she snatched the toy from his hand and buried her face back in her mother's neck.

Several feet of air separated them but Gwen could still literally *feel* his big body clench and still. His intimidating concentrated maleness was even more pronounced than normal as the tension stretched the skin tight against his incredible bone structure. His eyes swivelled from her hand cradling the back of Ellie's head to her face.

It felt like years before he spoke but it was probably only seconds, his voice low and soft. He seemed unaware that he was speaking Spanish and, while she only had a schoolgirl smattering of the language, Gwen didn't need a dictionary to translate the stream of hoarse words.

He knew—of *course* he knew!

You'd have to be wilfully blind or stupid not to see what had drained the vibrant colour from his olive-toned face and dissolved his habitual aura of cool command.

He was seeing the same thing she had the moment she'd looked into her newborn baby's face. Previous to that day she had gone along with loving new parents who said their baby was the spitting image of one or other parent, while in her experience the soft infant features all looked alike.

But Ellie's baby face had borne a startling likeness to Rio from day one. She'd tried to tell herself that the likeness would lessen as the little girl got older, but seeing them to-gether now dispelled that vain hope. If any-thing, being able to study their faces side by side made the likeness between father and daughter all the more striking.

He wouldn't need a DNA test to confirm his fatherhood this time, she thought bitterly. It was practically like looking in a mirror for him. It was all in the bones, the angle of the jaw, the hairline, the shape of Ellie's forehead and, most of all, her eyes, fringed by a double row of sooty eyelashes.

'The child…she is mine.' He sounded as shocked as he looked for a man who'd pre-sumably been there and done this before. But maybe it was easier to deal with the facts on paper rather than be confronted with a real-life person. For all she knew he might never have even seen his son.

Or he might be with, or even have married, the mother of his firstborn. Both were equally possible, she realised with a rush of shock.

Strangely she found the latter possibility more disturbing and her feelings could not be totally explained away by her natural sadness for the things his firstborn would have that Ellie wouldn't—like the love of his father.

She couldn't take her eyes off the muscle clenching and unclenching in his concave cheek. It didn't even cross her mind to lie—what would be the point now?

'Yes, she is yours. Her name is Ellie and she's just two.'

She could see he was struggling to string a sentence together and waited, stomach clenched, for what he might say next.

'Does your husband know the truth or does he think she is his?'

Her delicate jaw clenched as she eyed him with disdain. If she'd had a free hand she might have forgotten she was a committed pacifist—*again!*—and slapped his face! The question of why something about this man had bypassed a few thousand years of evolution and made her feel primal was for another time.

'Your opinion of me is so flattering, as always.' So not only was she the woman who went through his private correspondence, now she was the woman who pretended another man's child was her husband's. 'But I don't actually have a husband. All female staff here are referred to as Mrs, regardless of marital status.'

He dismissed the explanation with an impatient shake of his dark head. 'But you said—'

Her chin lifted to a challenging angle. 'Actually,' she countered, '*I* didn't say anything, you just assumed. Hush, Ellie, darling,' she murmured, and brushed a strand of dark hair back from her daughter's flushed forehead as the sharp voices made her start to cry again.

'You allowed me to think—'

'I don't owe you any explanations,' she hissed back quietly between clenched teeth for the sake of her fretful, feverish daughter. She really didn't have the time or energy to deal with his indignation or anger right now.

His eyes were on the poorly child who had settled a little now, and the expression in those dark depths was almost hungry. Gwen experienced a spasm of gut-clenching fear. Suddenly, for the very first time she encountered the possibility that he might *want* Ellie. He might actually want to take Ellie away from her.

'I think explanations are the least you owe me,' he intoned grimly, equally quietly.

She closed her eyes and gave her head a tiny

shake of disbelief, the anger spilling through her pushing away the last vestiges of guilt. 'I owe you nothing and you owe me nothing. We are simply two people who...who...collided.'

Rio's eyes lifted to hers. 'Several times,' he murmured, the brief wicked gleam in his eyes fading as he struggled to clear the sound of a child crying that was still echoing in his head. It was disconcerting as the echo was playing in sync with the real thing.

The child...*his* child—and would that ever seem real to him?—had begun to sob and squirm in her mother's arms. As his focus widened beyond his own private drama involving the three of them, he became aware for the first time that they were beginning to attract attention. Some of the pupils and staff filing out of the hall had slowed to stare at them curiously.

'I can't believe that we are having this conversation.'

'What did you think would happen?' he bit out.

Colour stinging her cheeks, Gwen rebutted, 'What I mean is this was not supposed to happen.'

'What, getting pregnant, or me finding out I had a child?'

'Both,' she admitted removing a hank of her hair from his daughter's—*Ellie's*—tenacious grip.

'I'm no expert, but shouldn't you be taking her to the hospital?' He knew nothing about children but this one was...*his daughter*. He gave his dark head a shake, but, no, he was actually awake and this was really happening. It wasn't a dream. The shock he was experiencing was momentarily blanked out by a fresh wave of anger as he thought of all the moments he had missed with his child that he would never get back.

'That's right, you're *not* an expert,' Gwen pointed out. When had he last had a sleepless night? she thought, her contempt almost immediately vanishing to be replaced by a sick feeling in the pit of her stomach as she recalled some of the things Rio usually thought preferable to sleep.

It was a measure of how completely he took over her mind that this thought led seamlessly into an image imprinted and preserved in her head in perfect detail, the moment captured for ever, along with the nameless ache she had felt deep inside as she'd stared at him lying asleep on his back early one morning, one arm above his head, his face in repose. The lines that might one day be permanent had been ironed out, looking, not softer, exactly, but younger beneath the piratical stubble that emphasised the angles of his jaw and the hollow of his carved cheeks.

In the soft dappled early morning light that had filtered through the blinds on the open window, his skin had shone like dull gold against the crumpled white sheet that was bunched across his narrow hips, the shadows emphasising the muscular definition of his chest and ridged belly.

She remembered desperately wanting to touch him and so she had, her fingers moving along the line of dark hair that ran down his belly until her hand was caught and she found herself staring into black, wickedly gleaming and not at all sleepy eyes that were still looking at her as he pulled her down on top of him.

Breaking free of the vivid memories drew a tiny grunt of effort from her parted lips.

'This is neither the time nor the place for this

conversation,' she said, a shade of desperation creeping into her voice because there was no time and no place where she wanted to have this conversation.

He glanced towards their growing audience. Clearly, it was the first thing they had agreed on. 'So where, and when?'

She looked at him in horror, the recognition dawning in her brain that there was going to be no escape route, no secret door, no alternative to them having a face-to-face discussion.

She tipped her head in acknowledgement and defeat. 'All right, my cottage.'

'Cottage?' His slightly confused expression cleared. 'The one in the grounds you mentioned? Right, I will find it.' He glanced at his watch. 'Shall we say five o'clock?'

Gwen shook her head. 'No, six.' By that time she ought to have been able to pacify Ellie and if not he'd just have to wait. She lifted her chin. Her daughter would always come first with her and the sooner he caught onto that fact, the better. The world might work around Rio Bardales's schedule but she had moved on.

## CHAPTER FOUR

GWEN NOTICED ABSENTLY that her hand was shaking as she tried to coax her daughter to take the temperature-lowering medicine. When the toddler turned her head away for the fourth time and it spilled down her front Gwen felt the tears she'd so far held back begin to spill down her cheeks.

Taking a deep breath, she squeezed her eyes tight shut and told herself, *Self-pity, Gwen, is really not attractive.*

A moment later as she choked back a sob and forced a smile, perhaps her change of attitude communicated itself to her child, who stopped crying to watch her mother with big eyes.

Gwen took advantage of the moment of calm to spoon the mixture between her lips. 'Excellent, good girl...'

She sat back with a sigh as a wave of love so strong that it made her breathless washed over her. Before Ellie had been born she had worried about bonding with her, not able to imagine this swell of instinctive parental love. Suddenly, an image of Rio's face, the shock of recognition in his eyes when he'd seen Ellie, surfaced in her head.

What would it feel like to be hit by the reality you were a father that way? The truth was she could not imagine that scenario any more than she could imagine how he was feeling now he'd had time to take it on board.

Or maybe he was wondering how to break the news to the mother of his son—his partner…his wife? Her life had moved on and it was only reasonable to assume that his had too.

*Which* Rio would arrive? Would he be angry? Cold? Businesslike?

Would he even arrive?

Another image flashed in front of her, of the expression in his dark eyes as he had stared at Ellie, and she shivered. It was definitely not the look of a man who had any intention of walking away.

Trying to shake the feeling of impending doom that weighed her down, she told herself her time would be better spent preparing a plan of action for a scenario that was never meant to happen.

She tried to reawaken the feeling of optimism, of liberation almost, that she'd felt the day Ellie was born and she had come to her decision not to tell Rio, a decision that had nothing to do with the months of arguing with herself and playing devil's advocate. The decision had been made because it felt right, and she could finally move on as a mother. It was a new, exciting and scary chapter in her life, but she could do it. Alone.

She didn't need Rio's help, and she was not going to beg or humiliate herself by submitting to DNA testing. She had mentally wiped him out of her life. Well, to be completely truthful, it had been a work in progress but she'd been getting there.

Sadly he didn't get the same memo!

With Ellie on her shoulder, she began to pace up and down the small cosy living room humming softly, and after a few grumpy kicks and moans Ellie settled, soothed by the rhythmic motion. Gwen carried on humming, glancing at the clock on the mantle occasionally until she felt the toddler go limp in her arms and the baby breaths become deep and even.

She pushed open the only bedroom door with her foot. The lack of a second bedroom was one of those problems that she had left for the future, as for the moment the cot at the bottom of her bed worked and there was room for a small bed later on.

Pulling back the sheet, she laid her sleeping daughter down. Her cheeks were rosy but no longer feverish as the medicine was doing its job. Switching on the baby monitor even though there wasn't anywhere in the tiny cottage where she wouldn't hear her cry, Gwen drew the curtains and crept from the room, leaving the door ajar behind her.

Back in the living room, she glanced at the clock again, silently counting the minutes until Rio would appear. It was hard to rehearse what she was going to say when she didn't have a clue what he was going to ask, or demand or… She sighed and began to chew her plump bottom lip distractedly, fighting her way free of another wave of despair.

'For goodness' sake, Gwen, stop feeling sorry for yourself!'

Her eyes narrowed with determination as she began to whisk around the room, plumping the odd cushion, picking up a toy and lobbing it in the toy box beside the window. Yesterday she had been wishing she had the space for a playroom; today she loved everything exactly the way it was. Perhaps you had to have your little world threatened to appreciate a worn carpet or a shower that was only a frustrating trickle.

It was a struggle to visualise Rio in these surroundings; it really was *not* his natural environment. He was sleek and exclusive and— she released a quivering sigh—just the *thought* of him being here had the power to make her insides quiver. Shameful though it was, it hardly seemed worth the energy it cost pretending she wasn't still as vulnerable as she had ever been to his lethal sexuality.

It just proved that sexual chemistry was utterly indiscriminate. Ignoring the butterfly kicks still making their presence known in her stomach, she walked into her diminutive galley kitchen to get a glass of water to moisten her suddenly dry mouth.

It was the uncertainty, she told herself, that

was really testing her. If Rio had gone into denial mode she could have dealt with it, or at least dealt with it more easily. Of course, he might still go that way once he had got over the initial shock.

He might just want confirmation that she was not going to make any future demands on him. Well, she could happily give him that—she'd sign anything if it meant he'd leave them in peace.

Gwen tiptoed back into the bedroom, checked on Ellie, who was sleeping peacefully still, and jumped at the sound of a rose branch scratching the window as the freshening breeze caught it.

*You need to relax, Gwennie girl*, she told herself, before grinning at the sheer impossibility of this. Absently fishing a lip gloss from her pocket, she smeared it over her lips before closing the door behind her.

By the time she had sat down and then jumped up again she had chewed the strawberry moisture off.

Would he be on time?

Should she have contacted a lawyer?

As if she had one on speed dial! She gave a

small snort of self-mocking laughter and tried not to think of the access to top legal experts that Rio had.

Discovering a stray brightly coloured building block behind a cushion that had escaped her whirlwind round of frenzied tidying, she headed for the overflowing toy box when the knock on the door made her leap like a startled deer.

She took a deep breath and schooled her features into neutrality, or as close as she was going to get to that, and opened the door. Her eyes travelled upwards as she took a half-step outside, her elbow brushing the roses around the door.

His jacket had gone and the fabric of his tailored shirt was fine enough to suggest the drifts of body hair on his torso. Or maybe she was just seeing them because she knew they were there. Her cheeks heated guiltily at the thought.

'You live here?'

She didn't pause to think of a sarcastic response, just nodded.

He didn't respond to the social cue so, after an awkward pause, she added, 'It's convenient.' Less convenient was noticing for the first time the coiled tension in his lean body. It wasn't just his masculinity that sent a fresh shudder through her body, it was the predator barely disguised by the perfect tailoring.

One dark brow lifted but he still didn't say anything. Gwen tried to ignore the grab of some emotion that felt like a hand in her chest as their eyes finally connected, the moment she had been avoiding.

She wanted to look away but the moment dragged, hampered by the mind-fogging hormonal flare she felt. She resorted to stiff formality as she finally managed to slide her eyes to some point over his left shoulder. Sexual chemistry had no place here; she owed it to Ellie to keep a clear head. She had learnt from her mistakes and it was more important than ever not to repeat them.

*Chance would be a fine thing!*

Ignoring the shame-inducing reaction of her inner voice, she gave a faint smile. 'Come in.' She stood to one side and, after an equally stilted and blank-faced pause, he stepped past her directly into her sitting room.

In the confined space his sheer physicality

took on an extra resonance, as did the predatory undercurrents that had made her hormones leap.

Rio discovered that the cottage, which looked like a chocolate box outside, was more like a doll's house inside. He supposed it was charming if you liked low beams and leaded windows, but he didn't; he preferred light and space. His eyes moved over the toys spilling out of a box in the corner and they darkened. He was still desperately struggling to assimilate the knowledge he was a father, but the emotions were so complex and intertwined that the anger kept colliding with the shock and the sheer gut-wrenching wonder of it all.

It was a situation that he'd not asked for but one he was certainly responsible for, which equated to this combined anger and guilt. Being a father was one thing, but having the fact hidden from him, leaving him an outsider in a process he had been so intimately involved with, left him feeling...what, exactly?

Of course, the irony and the massive degree of hypocrisy his reaction generated was impossible to duck. How could he blame Gwen when he had done the very same thing to his brother? His twin, his other half, who still didn't know he had fathered a son... The guilt Rio had lived with every day since he'd agreed to the deception hadn't gone away, but it had been easier to bear because he had been so sure that he'd made the right decision.

Today's events made him feel far less secure about that. Had Gwen thought she'd made the right decision too?

Had she thought his daughter was better off not knowing her father? And could he really blame her? This degree of reluctant understanding of her possible motives didn't lessen his determination to be an ongoing part of this child's life, to be the best father he could, but the next step was convincing Gwen of this. Of course, his advantage in all this was that he suspected she had a strongly developed sense of fair play whereas he was quite *flexible* about such things, especially when the stakes were this high.

He had no intention of taking no for an answer.

He looked around the room again and glanced at her, wondering if she thought he considered it to be shabby and cramped. She was clearly bracing her shoulders in a defensive attitude and when he suddenly turned, she jumped, taking a nervy involuntary step backwards. She bit down, her white teeth sinking into her plump lower lip, distracting him for a moment. Then she cleared her throat loudly, and he wondered if she'd noticed.

Rio frowned. He could see that the blue-veined pulse at the base of her slender throat was throbbing nervously, and the possibility that she was scared of him made him feel like a monster.

'Are you all right?' he asked when she lowered her hand from her mouth.

She nodded. 'Can I get you anything to drink?' she offered.

'It sounds like *you* need a drink,' he said, wondering if that would relax her a little.

She shook her head.

'I'm okay, thanks.'

'Is she… *Ellie*…?' He paused after pushing out her name slowly as if he was still trying it out for fit. 'Is she feeling better now?' he asked, grimacing faintly as he heard the accusatory note edge into his tone. He could tell by the stiffening of her posture that Gwen had too.

She nodded.

'Can I see her?' His jaw clenched, the fine muscles quivering, as the request brought home just how wrong this situation was. He was asking permission to see his own child.

The look of alarm that flickered across her face as she desperately tried to think of an excuse to say no only added to the feeling of *wrongness*.

'I'm not going to snatch her, you know,' he said with impatient irony.

He saw a guilty flush rise up her neck until her face looked as if it were burning. 'I never thought you were,' she protested defensively.

His expressive mouth twisted. 'But you are now.' She was as easy to read as a neon headline.

'She's sleeping.'

For a guilty moment he acknowledged a flash of relief. How did you talk to a person who was little more than a baby? What did you say to your own child? But the hunger to see her again remained stronger than his self-doubt.

It made him think again of Roman, his twin, who had a child he would never know, and the guilt he lived with every day tightened as he promised huskily, 'I won't wake her.'

For a split second he thought she was going to refuse and the hell of it was there was not a thing he could do about it. He had fathered a child and yet he had no rights… His taut jaw clenched, dragging the skin tight across his slashing cheekbones at the prospect of having to beg to see his own child.

Gwen kick-started her brain, ashamed that for a few vital moments she had allowed herself to get sidetracked by the small jagged scar she had noticed on his forehead, white against his golden-toned skin.

'Fine,' she mumbled, except of course it wasn't. 'This way.'

She didn't look at him but she was very conscious of his physical presence as he followed her through the door she pushed open. She wondered where she drew the line—when did she say no? There had to be guidelines, limits…didn't there?

Gwen turned and saw straight away that his attention was almost immediately riveted by the cot that stood at the foot of the small old-fashioned brass double bed in the bright-yellow-painted room. She wondered if he could feel the quivering tension coming off her but she said nothing, just stood to one side as he walked towards the cot cautiously.

Gwen hung back, hands clenched, not wanting him here and particularly not wanting to see the conflict in his face as he looked down into the cot. Yet it was the wonder that flickered into his eyes, and something close to longing there too, that she really didn't want to see the most.

She looked away. She couldn't let this situation be all about him and his feelings. This was about her and Ellie; they were a unit of two. Rio had to stay on the outside of that unit—she'd be fair but firm and if necessary selfish in order to protect Ellie.

'I'll be just through there.' She nodded her head to indicate the other room and left, but she didn't think he noticed.

It was five minutes before he joined her. Gwen was staring out of the window blindly and didn't hear his soft-footed approach. It was only the prickling on the back of her neck that alerted her to his presence.

She turned and saw him standing just inside the doorway, but his expression told her nothing. 'Sorry, I didn't hear—'

'I didn't wake her...' he said at the same time, and hesitated. Then, as she stayed silent, he added, 'Is she well?' He dragged a hand through his dark hair and moved further into the room. 'What did the doctor say?'

'She hasn't seen a doctor.' Before he could express the outrage she could see tauten his face she quickly explained, 'The next appointment the surgery has is not for several days.'

Rio snarled out his opinion of this situation in a flood of blistering angry Spanish.

'Do you mind translating that?' she asked, bewildered.

His jaw clenched. 'That's outrageous!'

She accepted the more polite, shortened version, noticing with a shiver that he suddenly seemed even taller and more physically intimidating in the small room.

'What's the doctor's number?'

Her eyes flew wide in alarm. 'What do you think you're doing?'

He flashed her a look as he pulled his phone from his pocket. 'What do you think? Should I call him out? Or, better still, I'll tell him you need a second opinion—except you haven't even had a first—'

Feeling her temper spurt at the implied criticism, she cut him off, her voice cold but controlled. 'For the record *he* is a *she* and this isn't your call to make in any sense of the word.'

She could see him almost literally bite back a sharp retort as her words sank in. Instead he threw her a look that simply seethed with frustration.

She struggled not to empathise with how he must be feeling, but she couldn't afford to allow herself to soften towards him or show him any weakness, or very soon it could be Rio telling her when she could see her daughter.

This horrifying image hardened her resolve.

Rio already had a child, she just had Ellie.

'You may have been a parent longer than me.' She saw his blank expression and tacked on sarcastically, 'Or had you already forgotten?'

He didn't respond verbally to that barb, but at

least she'd got some reaction. She supposed it was *something* that he could clearly feel guilt, always supposing she wasn't misreading the reason for the dark bands of colour across his high cheekbones.

'But *I've* been doing this for two years now,' she added with quiet dignity. No point explaining that sometimes she still didn't feel as though she knew what she was doing. She was not about to tell him about her insecurities; it would feel a lot like handing more ammunition to someone who already had a gun aimed at your head.

A frown flickered across her face at the over-dramatic analogy—she *really* had to lower the levels of paranoia. On the other hand she really couldn't see a downside to Rio thinking she was an expert in child-rearing.

The seething silence lengthened while their eyes clashed, black on iridescent blue. The dark bands of colour scoring his cheekbones deepened and his eyes dropped as he finally slid the phone slowly back into his pocket, tacitly admitting a defeat she could see was alien to his nature and life experience.

'And that is my fault, I suppose,' he said bitterly.

Gwen recognised that this could easily escalate into some sort of war of attrition. One of them had to keep their temper, so she took hers tightly in hand and shook her head. If she lost it she might say things that she would undoubtedly later regret.

'I didn't say that. I'm simply saying that being a mum is a learning process and this isn't the first time Ellie has been unwell. Babies do sometimes become unwell and they can't exactly tell you what's wrong!' Belatedly aware that her voice had climbed shrilly and started to wobble, she took a deep, calming breath.

He didn't need to know about her doubts, about the nights she longed for someone to share the responsibility that came with being the parent of a baby, but there hadn't been anyone so she had made the unilateral decision that she no longer needed any help.

'Her temperature has already come back down. She had a cold last week and it's left her a little stuffed up. She's been pulling at her ear…she seems a bit prone to ear problems.'

She pushed out the information quickly before explaining something no new parent, or indeed anyone who had never been ill, would know. 'They are reluctant to give antibiotics these days for something that is probably viral, and sitting in a crowded waiting room was not going to make her feel any better. They'd just tell me to take her home and do what I am already doing.'

'Which is?'

He listened in silence as she explained that she'd given Ellie medicine to lower her temperature and made sure she had plenty of fluids.

'And sleep,' she added, 'is really good, though she's likely to be a bit grumpy when she wakes up.' She really hoped this would be sorted and he'd be gone by the time Ellie woke up, but, being a realist, she could see that this might be optimistic, so it was best to prepare him for the worst. 'Or then again, she might be chirpy. It's not an exact science...'

'But in general she is a healthy child?'

Gwen was relieved he sounded calmer. 'She's fine and, yes, she's had no health problems beyond the usual.'

He nodded and she could see from the blank look on his face that he didn't have a clue what the usual was. Perhaps he didn't have much to do with his son?

'Right, then, is there anything else you'd like to know?' She paused, wondering if she should tell him straight off that she wasn't going to make any financial demands on him. Just cut the polite and painfully awkward chit-chat and get to the point?

'This must have been a shock for you,' she said, remembering how much of a shock it had been to her to discover she was pregnant.

She'd run home—that had been her first mistake.

Ironic really that her parents, who had never really believed in her five-year plan and her career, had suddenly been absolutely emphatic that she not give it up. Her father, they'd said, had already told everyone at the golf club about her success, and they were impressed— as if this clinched the argument. Except she wasn't arguing, she was just letting them talk at her, feeling her heart freeze over as she listened to them in increasing horror.

'So you want me to "get rid of it"?' She

remembered hearing her father's hiss of exasperation as she sketched sarcastic inverted commas in the air and finished, 'Just so that you can continue to have bragging rights at the golf club?'

'Well, you've finally done something for us to be proud of.'

Ironically, once her parents' pride in her would have mattered so much; it was what she'd been striving for all her life.

'Gwen, dear, you must see your life will be ruined. All your plans will come to nothing—and what will people say?'

'And that's what really matters, isn't it? What people think! The only thing that matters to you is appearances. There is no disgrace, no shame involved, in having a baby alone these days, Mam.' Gwen's glance flickered towards the towering presence of disapproval that was her father. 'But there is plenty of shame in living a lie.'

Unable to meet her eyes, her mother looked away and whispered, 'I only want what's best for you, *cariad*.'

'I know, Mam, but—'

'How dare you talk to your mother like that? And don't call her Mam—it's common!'

As he planted a beefy arm around his wife's shoulders Gwen found herself wondering when she'd last seen any display of physical affection between them.

'If you keep it, we want nothing to do with you.'

Gwen looked at her mother, who just shook her head and looked away.

It was the exact point when Gwen knew she was totally on her own.

Her mum looked small, like someone who'd had the life sucked out of her. Gwen knew that at one time her mother would have been strong enough to resist her father's demands that Gwen get rid of her baby...and her mother was probably paying a silent price ever since for not standing up to him, but she'd had no more fight left.

Gwen shook off the heavy empty feeling that came with the unhappy memories and forced a smile.

'Do you want to sit down? Oh, not that one,' she added quickly, gesturing at the overstuffed armchair he was standing next to. 'The legs are a bit wobbly.'

He probably thought the whole place was a *bit wobbly*. After all, he had just been escorted on a tour around the school, including state-of-the-art laboratory facilities, where no expense had been spared. Despite this, the employees lived in accommodation that could only be called basic.

He shook his head and walked across to the second armchair but, instead of sitting, stood behind it and placed his hands on the back rest. 'I'm fine.'

Gwen assumed his dark brooding scowl was directed at his surroundings and lifted her chin. Ah, well, it would do him good to slum it, she decided, struggling to hold onto her angry contempt as an image of his *cottage* on the Cape Cod island off Martha's Vineyard flashed into her head. When he'd first asked her to dinner, she'd assumed he was staying in a hotel, but she had learnt that it was never a good idea to *assume* with Rio.

His version of a cottage was the incredible sprawling seafront property set in the middle of lush, beautifully tended acres. The fact they had arrived in a private plane that he'd piloted himself should have been a clue to how ridiculously wealthy he was, but the sight of his house—or, more correctly, his estate—had brought it home to her for the first time that she was dealing with someone who lived in a completely different world.

A world where *wonky* had no place, just as she'd had no place in his.

She absently smoothed a throw that she had positioned to hide the worn patch on the arm of a chair. This was her world, hers and Ellie's, and she was not ashamed of it, she was *proud* of what she had achieved with no help from anyone and she wouldn't allow him to make her feel any different about it.

For years she'd watched her father blame her mother, or even sometimes her, every time he'd strayed—which had been often. But it had always been their fault for not understanding him, for not being *enough* for him.

The moment Ellie was born Gwen had vowed that she'd be a good role model. That her daughter would never have to feel ashamed of her the way Gwen had eventually become ashamed of her mother, who had been unable to break free of the cycle of emotional abuse doled out by her father.

Ellie would never feel that she was not *enough*!

# CHAPTER FIVE

RIO WATCHED GWEN STRAIGHTEN, the cushion she had picked up still pressed to her chest protectively, her expression distant but wary as she focused on him. The idea that she felt she needed to protect herself from him made the muscles along his jaw quiver.

He admired the way she'd made this small house into a home, despite its worn appearance. He thought less of the school's headmaster, not Gwen. The employer in him considered this bad working practice. Loyalty was a two-way street; you treated staff well and they in turn were willing to go the extra mile.

The newly discovered father in him found the idea of his child not enjoying the luxuries that he took for granted felt wrong on so many levels. His child, but except for today's chance encounter he might have walked past her in the street and not known her!

'Why didn't you tell me, Gwen?'

Thrown by the directness of the question, she blinked. 'It was my decision to go ahead with the pregnancy, my body, my baby,' she intoned solemnly. 'What would have been the point telling you? What were you going to do, after, of course, I'd submitted to a lie detector and the prescribed range of DNA tests? Marry me?'

He winced but she didn't notice.

'People marry for less,' he observed carefully.

'Love, you mean?'

'You think a transitory chemical attraction is more important than having a child together?'

'You make love sound like a selfish indulgence,' she said.

He arched a strongly delineated brow. 'I wasn't talking about maternal love.'

'You asked what I think, well, I think that Ellie and what is best for her are the most important things to me,' she told him fiercely.

'Until you meet a man?' His broad shoulders tensed as a flash freeze image formed in his head of a faceless male in Gwen's bed and being a father to his child. The constant tug of sexual attraction he was fighting paled beside this raw and primal response to what was only an imaginary scenario.

She released a scornful laugh. 'Because I feel incomplete without a man in my life? Hardly! I have Ellie, and my work, so I already have everything I need.'

But did she have enough money? he wondered.

'I suppose that contacting you to keep you in the loop was an option, but not one that filled me with joy and positivity after our affair ended the way it did. And quite honestly I was too busy throwing up for several months to worry about it that much.'

He felt a kick of guilt that was totally irrational because he hadn't known she'd suffered that badly, but, as they said in every courtroom drama, ignorance was no defence. Something twisted inside him at the thought of her being alone and suffering.

But she wouldn't have been alone, he realised with a sense of relief. Not all families were as dysfunctional as his.

'You went home?' As his glance drifted over her sinuous curves, it was hard for him to imagine her heavily pregnant.

Gwen's eyes lowered. 'For a time,' she said, moistening her lips. 'I had some savings.'

'You packed in your job right off? I'm sure they had a very generous healthcare plan.'

'I was living in America and I was still on a probationary period, so there was no way they were going to give me a permanent contract if I was pregnant.'

He cleared his throat and gave a thoughtful nod. 'So not good timing, then.'

She gave a sudden laugh. 'There's never a good time to have a baby and yet people still do.'

He would have found this conversation more comfortable if he'd been the target of her resentment and anger, but she appeared remarkably calm about having her life thrown upside down. 'This was hardly a planned pregnancy.'

'The statistics on that make interesting reading—fewer than you'd think are planned.'

'At least you had a support network back home.'

Gwen said nothing. The less said about her *support network*, the better. She smoothed back her hair and gave a casual shrug.

'I have friends and I like to be independent.

Also, as luck would have it, I had a small win on a premium bond my late godmother bought me years ago, so money wasn't a problem.' It was important to her not to come across as a victim—not of anything. 'Look, I'm sure you're not really interested in my finances, so let's just get to the real reason you're here.'

Something flickered at the backs of his eyes as he arched a sardonic brow. 'And that would be?' he prompted with a display of gentle interest, though there was nothing anyone would describe as gentle in the headlight stare that she found uncomfortably intent.

'I am not going to make any demands on you. I don't expect any involvement from you at all.'

A nerve in Rio's cheek clenched. She said it as though he needed reassurance, while her attitude strongly suggested that the news that she didn't expect him to be any part of his own child's life was meant to make him *happy*! *Dios!* He would have been the first to concede that he might have given her reason to think he was not exactly a saint, but did she really think he was such a rat as to walk away from his own child?

'What sort of demands are we talking?' He kept his face locked in a mask of polite indifference that became increasingly hard to maintain as an image of her making some very pleasant demands of him floated through his head, her soft, husky laugh, her long, extremely flexible legs, her lips. His gaze sank to her mouth, which he assumed was about to say something far less pleasing than, *Again, please, Rio*!

His indolent drawl had nothing to do with the flames flickering in his mesmeric eyes, and for a moment Gwen lost her verbal footing as waves of distracting heat thrummed through her body.

She stammered out, 'I-I'll put it in writing if you want…? I expect you have lawyers on speed dial?' She faltered, her voice drying up as she encountered his furious glare. She could literally *feel* the anger vibrating off him.

'You think that's why I'm here? To have you sign some sort of nondisclosure agreement and pay you off!'

'I don't want your money. I don't want anything from you!' she exclaimed in horror, pushing aside a small voice in the back of her head that asked if she was allowing her pride to get in the way of Ellie's best interests.

But she was getting ahead of herself. Rio hadn't offered her anything yet, with strings or otherwise.

He sighed and dragged a hand through his hair, his eyes flicking to the half-closed bedroom door. 'It appears as if you're coping.'

As he gave the grudging concession—perhaps it was even a compliment?—her shocked, widened eyes flew to his face. But the expression in his own hooded gaze as he continued talking had her quickly back-pedalling on the compliment idea.

'But why should my daughter have to just *cope*? I realise it can't have been easy for you.'

Not even slightly mollified by the acknowledgement, Gwen ground her even white teeth. 'I'm not a victim.'

'I didn't mean to suggest that you are.'

She looked at him sideways and thought, *Yeah, not much?*

'I have a job I love, a daughter I adore—I consider myself extremely lucky.'

Rio's slender grip on diplomacy slipped through his fingers as he ground out a frustrated imprecation. This woman really was the most aggravating and touchy female he had ever encountered.

'Well, you would say that, wouldn't you, because you're too damned stubborn and independent to admit you needed help, even if your life depended on it, but this isn't just your life, is it? It's Ellie's, my daughter's...' He caught the flare in her eyes but ignored a stab of guilt for his below-the-belt blow. He still had a point to make. 'Our daughter does not even have a room of her own and she is left in the care of those who, although I am sure they are admirable, are little more than strangers...'

'Not to me!' she countered. 'And sometimes a child is better off with a stranger than a real parent.'

'You think my daughter would be better off with a stranger than me,' Rio said flatly.

Her blue eyes flew wide. 'That wasn't what I meant.' She heaved out a sigh and lifted her hands, palm up, as she admitted, 'I didn't have the best relationship with my father.'

His clenched air of tension relaxed somewhat at her admission. 'And now?'

'There is no relationship at all.'

He tipped his head but to her obvious relief didn't push it, instead murmuring a soft, expressionless, 'It happens.'

'Look, this could get very complicated. You already have a child and—' Something flashed in his eyes and she stumbled to a halt. 'Obviously your relationships are none of my business, and if you wanted to put something to one side for Ellie when she's older, for her university education, that might be a nice gesture.'

His head reared back, his high cheekbones standing out on a face that was rigid with offence, which she clearly found bewildering if the confused look on her face was anything to go by.

'You think I make a habit of impregnating women and walking away?' And why shouldn't she? he thought bitterly. After all, that was exactly what he had done, even if he'd only done it the once, rather than twice, as she believed.

Rio was not a person who had ever felt the need for the good opinion of others and he rarely, if ever, explained himself to anyone.

Some people called him arrogant and he was fine with that—people took him at his word or they didn't, and it was not something he ever lost sleep over.

So it came as a shock to have to fight the impulse to tell Gwen the truth about his brother's child, but it was not his secret to share and he had given his word to Marisa. It was a promise he couldn't break, even if he had regretted making it many times.

He sometimes wondered if the agreement with Marisa and his guilt over that had been partly responsible for the intangible distance that had grown between him and his twin. There was no question in his mind that, despite the kick in the gut that it had been at the time, he still hadn't accepted his brother's out-of-the-blue decision to walk away from the responsibilities they'd shared controlling the Bardales empire.

'I have no idea what sort of arrangement you have with—'

Rio cut across her, choosing his words with care. 'That child you speak of is not in my life.'

'I suppose fatherhood is not for everyone,' she muttered, looking at her feet.

'Your efforts to be non-judgemental could do with some work,' he said drily.

Her eyes flew to his face. 'I'm not judgemental,' she said huffily.

His eyes narrowed on her flushed, angry and quite heart-stoppingly beautiful face and he felt his blood heat with inconvenient but inevitable lust. 'I'm sure you're the epitome of tact and political correctness.'

'Things nobody is going to accuse you of!' she fired back.

His sensual lips twisted into a smile. 'Well, at least we've stopped being painfully polite to one another.'

'*I* am polite.'

'I'm starting to get the idea that you'd be happier if I wanted to escape my responsibilities.'

'I…we are not anyone's *responsibility*—' She stopped mid angry flow, her eyes widening to their fullest extent as she stared at him in dawning horror. 'You mean you're not?'

'What do you think I've been trying to say?'

'I won't know until you say it.'

'I want to co-parent Ellie. I want to be fully involved in her life.'

'Co-parent?' she parroted as though the word made no sense to her. 'You *want* to be involved?'

'Why are you so shocked? I may not have given birth to her, but half that child's make-up is mine.'

Gwen's bubble of laughter was half a sob. 'That's hard to miss.' She shook her head. 'But you have said that you don't have contact with your son so I assumed—'

'You mean you hoped?' he said cynically.

Her eyes slid away from his.

'Look, I'm not going to force you into anything. I just want to get to know my daughter and I think you owe me that at least.'

Any brownie points his placatory manner might have won was clearly cancelled out by that *owe* and he could see Gwen's temper fizz. '*Owe?* So are you keeping some sort of score card? You know, you might think I'm dim, but I can't for the life of me think what I could possibly owe you!'

'Ellie's first steps?'

He watched an arrested expression steal

across her face. She was so easy to read that he wondered how she'd got this far without someone taking advantage of her.

*She hadn't. Because you did.*

'First smile,' he ground out, pushing away the guilt. 'First word… In fact, you owe me for all the things I have already missed, all the milestone moments that I will never experience!'

The emotion that thickened his normally slight Spanish accent obviously shocked her deeply.

'I didn't think you'd want to experience them.' Honesty rang out in her voice.

'I have told you I want to be a part of her life. I meant it.'

Rio paused, tilting his head to shield the expression that flashed into his dark eyes as the dark irony struck home. He was fighting for a role that he had colluded with another to deprive his twin of.

He tensed, ready to quash the guilt and nagging doubts that inevitably accompanied the acknowledgement of his role in the deception, given an added knife twist now that he had discovered he was a secret father too.

But the two situations were different, he reasoned. Roman's relationship with the mother of his child had been over long before she had come to Rio asking for his help.

*You never had a relationship with Gwen, though*, the voice in his head contributed unhelpfully. *You just had sex.*

His jaw clenched. He did not need reminding about the sex. He remembered every touch, every gasp, every soft sigh… With an effort he dragged his thoughts away from the warm distractions filling it and focused on the facts that had influenced his decision.

The mother of his brother's child had approached Rio at a time when every media outlet had been delivering a new image of Roman, a now famous bestselling author who was as daring and handsome as his fictional hero on an almost daily basis. In every image the same woman was with him, frequently gazing lovingly up at him. His twin was happy, or appeared to be, with another woman. His life had clearly moved on.

Had Rio's own ever really moved on from the short torrid affair with Gwen?

The furrow between his ebony brows deepened as he closed down the inner dialogue. Not being in a relationship didn't meant that he hadn't moved on from Gwen; not being in a relationship meant he was doing something right. Living his life the way he always did.

A fleeting image of his brother's ex-lover floated into his head. Despite his initial natural inclination to side with his twin, Marisa's story and her genuine desperation had touched him, and brought home how far he and his twin had grown apart. There had been a time when they discussed everything.

He asked himself what would be achieved by telling Roman now. At the time, he couldn't for the life of him see anything positive in doing so. But his eyes drifted to the half-open door behind which his own child lay asleep and he realised that now his reaction might have been very different. But that had been then, he told himself, once more squashing down his guilt. Marisa's child had got the bone marrow he'd so desperately needed to save his life and that was what mattered the most.

'And every child deserves a father?'

He arched a brow, wondering if he had imagined the tense undercurrent in her question. 'You don't think so?'

'It depends on the father. If I think that you're not good for Ellie, I will cut off all access and I don't care if you have a tribe of lawyers throwing money at it.' Her eyes shot blue warning fire at him.

His lips twitched at her ferocious tigress act, except of course it wasn't an act. He was pretty sure she'd make anyone who hurt her child regret living. 'That seems reasonable.'

Suspicious of Rio's sudden, easy capitulation, Gwen folded her arms across her heaving breasts. 'So how do you envisage this working?' She was pleased she sounded calm and businesslike, and glad he couldn't hear the panicked thud of her heart. Although maybe he could—it was pretty much all she could hear.

Gwen couldn't help wondering if Rio was secretly regretting having no contact with his son and whether Ellie was going to be some sort of consolation prize. But as much as she hated the idea, Gwen knew that he was right to ask for the opportunity to get to know his daughter. She *owed* him a chance, at least, to establish some sort of paternal relationship with Ellie.

'I understand there is a week left of term and then you have a long summer vacation?'

She nodded cautiously. Even the most devoted staff were counting down the days.

'You have any plans?'

Gwen was not fooled for a moment by the seeming casualness of the question. 'I thought we might take a few trips to the beach. I might even buy a tent when Ellie is a bit older and try camping.' She had always wanted to camp when she was a child but her father had been too busy for family holidays and her mother came out in a rash at the idea of being that close to nature.

'That sounds enjoyable, but I have another idea, although I'm afraid it does not involve canvas. Come to Spain with me. I have a place with a private beach where you can relax and I can get to know my...*our* daughter,' he swiftly corrected in response to the warning flash from her eyes. 'And you can get used to me being part of your life.'

'You can't be a part of *my* life!' she snapped.

He arched a brow. 'Isn't that inevitable when

we have a child together? Don't make me fight you on this, Gwen.'

She found the absence of anything in his expression or voice more intimidating than if he'd yelled at her.

She swallowed, but her chin stayed lifted to a defiant angle. 'Are you threatening me?'

He gave an impatient shake of his head. 'Don't be so dramatic. I am simply telling you that I intend to be part of my child's life.'

'*Our* child's life.'

He smiled, all silky confidence and even white teeth. 'Exactly the point I have been trying to make.'

'I could send you reports...photos or—' Under the relentless unblinking gaze of his deep-set eyes her voice trailed off as she felt like a drowning man going under for the last time. 'Spain in the summer might be a little hot for Ellie and she can be quite fussy about her food.' The former was a relevant concern; the latter was a downright lie. Ellie happily munched through everything that was set in front of her.

'We have air conditioning and adequate sunscreen, plus she appears to have inherited my colouring…'

Her attention was immediately drawn to the vibrant deep gold of his skin. She shrugged while her treacherous hormones went wild as she struggled to dispel the image that seemed imprinted on her retinas of him standing in front of her naked, the formation of long bone and deep muscle giving him the look of a classic statue brought to warm, rampant life.

'It's hard to tell at this stage,' she mumbled.

'I have read that introducing children to new tastes early on influences healthy food preferences later on in life.'

Gwen wasn't sure that was completely true but it certainly sounded plausible, and while she was thinking about it, he added smoothly, 'So I will make the necessary arrangements and pick you both up on the last day of term. I'll be in touch soon to let you know what time.'

## CHAPTER SIX

RIO TRAVELLED LIGHT. Packing was not something that he wasted time and energy on. Like most things in life it all came down to good organisation.

That morning it had taken him five minutes between returning from his run, getting out of the shower and sliding suited and booted behind the wheel of his car, coffee cup in hand. His laptop and his bag containing all the essentials was slung in the boot of his car, a boot that up until about fifteen minutes ago had seemed capacious enough for his needs.

'Don't worry, we'll find Ant,' Gwen was saying to Ellie.

He knew it had been a mistake to get his hopes up. Struggling to cling onto his calm, he watched Gwen, holding the child by the hand, vanish back into the cottage…and ignored the odd twisting in his chest as the dark curly head tilted up to her mother.

The child said something that made Gwen pause before she dropped into a graceful stoop and swept the toddler up into her arms with practised ease.

He set his shoulders against the gatepost and wondered who Ant was. But he wasn't going to ask, because by now he was pretty sure this performance was all about making a point, just because he had arrived ten minutes earlier than they'd agreed in their email exchange. Gwen had already told him he couldn't come inside because they weren't quite ready.

He stood outside, feeling very much like a taxi driver with the meter running. It astonished him that a woman who could be totally calm in her professional life could be so disorganised when it came to getting one small child in a car.

Was she trying to show him that parenting was not all fun and games? Well, he'd never thought it was. Actually, it was not a subject that he'd spent much time thinking about—up until now.

Now he was thinking about it a lot, when he wasn't thinking about what he had done to his brother in depriving him of the opportunity to know his son. The rationalisation that he'd done it in good faith no longer worked, not since he had looked into his daughter's face and realised that blood really *was* thicker than water.

Guilt was his constant companion, and it was eating away at him, depriving him of a single moment's peace. It was sending him to the gym, where he'd worked himself into a sweat-soaked state of exhaustion in the hope of gaining some respite that deep down he didn't think he deserved.

What if he was as bad a father as he was a brother? His own father hadn't been a bad *father* as such, but he'd had little time for his sons because he had poured all the love he had to give on his wife. Or at the very least, it was his version of love—but it had been the kind of poisonous, stifling, controlling, jealous love that had made it a relief when she had finally summoned the courage to leave.

He wouldn't be like his father, that was the most important thing. So ever since he'd discovered Ellie, he'd read everything he could on the subject of parenting. He'd immersed himself in it, had pored over what people who were considered experts wrote about what made a good or bad parent until, frustrated by all the conflicting opinions, he had put the research aside.

Sometimes there was no replacement for hands-on experience, and he was about to be thrown in at the deep end. His eagerness was counterbalanced by a fear of failure that he had never encountered in his life before.

It was a new feeling for him and not one that he liked. Also, he could see no rational reason why he felt this way. It wasn't as if he didn't regularly put himself in positions outside his comfort zone. He believed in pushing himself to avoid becoming smug and stale, and he generally thrived on the exhilaration of new challenges.

All this attitude required was a belief in yourself, and Rio did. It didn't mean he didn't mess up on occasion, but he never stressed over the chance of this happening ahead of time, and if and when it did he never made the same mistake twice.

The problem was there were generally no second chances with parenthood and you weren't dealing with figures on a spreadsheet.

He knew that many would consider that there was pressure involved when a wrong move could wipe billions off a share value, a bad investment could make your brand toxic.

But those consequences paled into insignificance beside the possibility that something you did could harm your child.

'We're done!'

Finally! He relaxed his shoulders as Gwen appeared in the doorway, holding the toddler by the hand. She was wearing pale blue jeans that clung in all the right places, emphasising the long, sinuous length of her legs. Her tee shirt, tucked into a narrow red belt that emphasised the narrowness of her waist, was white with an abstract colourful print on the front.

The sunshine caught her chestnut hair, which she wore tied back from her face by a bright blue silk scarf, bringing out the incredible cobalt of her eyes.

'Oh, sorry, I forgot to check the fridge!'

He watched in disbelief as she opened the door, vanishing inside—*again*!

His teeth clenched as he silently counted to ten before crossing one shiny booted ankle over the other. He leaned against the gleaming paintwork of the low-slung limited-edition model and secured the open passenger door with his hand as a gust of wind caught it.

He glanced inside the car. The child seat now fitted in the back was not what he would have termed intuitive but he had eventually figured out the mechanism. It wasn't as though he hadn't had time. He flicked back his cuff to check out the watch on his wrist, beginning to wonder if she had some form of OCD... After all, how hard could it be to grab a suitcase and get a two-year-old out of the door?

'That's it, we're all set.'

Rio knew better this time and didn't get his hopes up.

Gwen revisited her mental checklist before she walked out of the front door, Ellie, clutching a plastic bucket in one hand and a spade in the other, trailing one step behind her.

'Beach now?' the little girl said for the tenth time in as many minutes.

Gwen tried very hard to be truthful with her daughter but this was not the time for a temper tantrum. So instead of correctly saying no, she smiled and opted for a distraction rather than a fib that would undoubtedly come back to bite her down the line, thanks to her daughter's very good memory.

'Oh, my, isn't that a big shiny car?' Gwen knew zero about cars but she knew what this wasn't and that was a family car. However, it was extremely shiny and no doubt eye-catching—much like its driver—to people who cared about such things.

It had probably cost as much as a small family house. Rio knew as little about the life normal people lived as he did parenting. She felt a tiny pang of guilt for taking some pleasure from the impatience he was struggling to disguise.

Ellie looked unimpressed. 'Want a twactor.' She turned to look at Rio, who was standing beside an open door concealing his impatience very badly. 'A pink one, or wed.'

'Red,' Gwen corrected automatically.

'Wed,' Ellie repeated obediently.

'Good girl,' Gwen said absently, trying not to breathe in the warm scent of Rio's skin that was making her stomach muscles quiver. This, she decided, stifling a deep sigh, was going to be a very long journey. She stood to one side to let Ellie climb into the narrow back seat. Leg room for rear passengers had clearly not been a priority for the designer.

'Climb in, sweetheart, and be careful of the seat.' Cream leather and small children were not a match made in heaven.

'Here, let me,' Rio offered.

'It's fine.' Gwen elbowed him away and, leaning inside, clicked the belt in place. 'There's a knack to it,' she said defensively when she straightened up.

Gwen and Rio got into the front seats and clicked their own belts into place.

'She's not car sick,' Gwen remarked as the car drew away.

'That's good to know,' Rio said gravely, despite the fact that she could tell he'd never even considered this factor.

'How far—?' she began then stopped, horror spreading across her face. There were still several cars parked on the grassy section that had been reserved for parents picking up boarders. Several of the latecomers were gathered in a huddle near the school gate chatting.

She froze for a second, then slid down the seat, ducking out of sight.

'Don't stop,' she hissed. 'Just drive past quickly. Go! Go!'

'Are you going to stay there for the entire journey with your head on my lap? I just feel I should warn you that being seen in that position might be...er...misinterpreted?' The image that flashed into her head at his remark instigated a slow-burn heat in her belly.

Struggling to ignore his silky observation, she eased herself back up in the seat she had just slithered down, pressing her spine against the leather backrest and feeling as mortified as it was humanly possible to feel.

'What do you mean?' she choked.

He arched a sardonic brow and she realised it *was* possible to feel more mortified. Her already hot face flamed with a fresh rush of embarrassed colour.

Once more in an upright position, she stared straight ahead at green hedgerows flashing by as she sat, hands clasped in her lap, waiting for him to say something sarcastic.

He didn't.

'I suppose you think that was funny,' she muttered.

She shot a look at his enigmatic profile and

looked away again quickly. Now she knew what a silence that spoke volumes sounded like.

'I thought everyone would already have left.' She could have kicked herself for being over-confident. The Harker parents were notorious for being late picking up their boys. She bit her lip. 'If I'd been a bit quicker on the uptake, we could have gone out the back gate.'

'Because being seen with me would be—?'

'Have you any idea how fast gossip travels in this place?'

'I know two-year-olds still believe that clos-ing their eyes makes them invisible, but...'

'You think they saw me?'

'I'd say that's a distinct possibility.'

She bent her head and covered her face with her hands. 'Oh, God I know they did and I looked straight at them too...it was just in-stinct.'

Rio had had women he'd never seen before literally fall at his feet to drape themselves all over him in order to sneak a selfie with him, some fainting theatrically so that he could catch them and they could see the image go viral on social media the next day, but to have a woman ashamed to be seen with him was something of a first for him.

Clearly if he wanted his ego kept in check, Gwen Meredith was the right person for the job.

'I take it you've not told anyone where you are spending your vacation?' he said drily.

'No.'

'So I am your dirty little secret. How… charming.'

'I'm a private person.'

'Surely that is being paranoid? Do you not think it's inevitable that the identity of your child's father will eventually become public, or would you like me to wear a false moustache, possibly a full beard?'

'I have to work with these people,' she protested.

'Actually, you don't,' he said pointedly.

'I need to work, Rio. I'm not rich.'

'But I am.'

The suggestion that she would allow him to keep her brought her head up. 'I intend to be a role model for my daughter. I want her to be proud of me.'

'You do not think that being a mother is a job to be proud of?'

'Yes…no…of course I do, but I need to work for my own self-respect.' She glanced behind a little nervously, but Ellie was busy holding a conversation in gibberish between a teddy bear and a toy horse.

He looked thoughtful but said nothing.

Then he commented, 'She seems to have an active imagination.'

'Most two-year-olds do.'

'And most two-year-olds…' Rio couldn't understand a word Ellie was saying right now but struggled to tactfully ask Gwen what he wanted to know without causing offence. 'Do they have much vocabulary?' he wondered casually.

'She is actually considered bright for her age.'

'Ah… I don't know many two-year-olds… or any, actually. So here we are.'

Gwen looked around as they drove through some tall gates. 'This is a private airstrip.'

'Yes, it avoids the congestion of the bigger airports and the facilities are quite good,' he explained as he drove directly onto the tarmac.

Her eyes widened. So this was flying, but not as she knew it.

Once he'd brought the car to a halt he jumped out and started to talk to a man who had come out of the nearest jet. A few minutes later Rio walked around the car and opened the passenger door.

'I have a couple of last-minute details to sort out.'

'With the plane?'

He shook his head. 'No, there is no problem with our flight; it's just work. Ramon will board you.' Like an actor in the wings waiting for his cue, a uniformed figure came hurrying across the tarmac. 'He will make you both comfortable and I will join you presently.'

He did, but only for a moment; the pilot, it seemed, was a friend of his and he chose to travel up front with him, having first checked that she and Ellie were all right.

'We're fine,' Gwen assured him, glad of a respite from the nerve-shredding effect of his close proximity, no matter how short.

The flight went without incident and, thanks to a very attentive crew, she didn't really have to deal with Ellie, who they seemed to enjoy entertaining, though by the time the jet circled to land night was falling and Ellie's eyelids were drooping.

By the time they were preparing to get into the car that waited for them, a big four-wheel drive with plenty of room, Ellie was sound asleep.

Gwen really hoped she stayed that way although she felt as though sleep might be a long time coming for herself. Gwen's body was still taut with anxiety and self-doubt as she had spent most of the journey staring out of the window into blackness, wondering what awaited them in Spain and asking herself if she had made the right decision bringing Ellie here.

But what other option had she had?

Did he *really* want to be part of Ellie's life? She frowned; there were far too many questions and no answers. The only thing she was sure of was that, even though her romantic fantasies about him had been shattered, she was still far from immune to his potent brand of masculinity.

'Let me help with—'

His deep voice jolted Gwen free of her introspection and back to the moment, and an instinct she didn't question made her lurch forward. She virtually elbowed her way past him to block his access to the sleeping child, but it wasn't all win, win... The fleeting collision had made the prickle under her skin even more intense.

How she was going to survive the constant exposure over the next few weeks to this permanent adrenaline overload, she had no idea.

'No, I can manage.' Wincing inwardly at the defensive quality in her own voice, she flashed him a quick look through her lashes.

She looked away quickly because he was standing uncomfortably close—was there even such a thing as comfortable when it came to him? From the electric effect he had on her nervous system she wasn't sure what the safety-zone perimeter was—or even if there was one.

She found her weakness to him disturbing, though not as disturbing as the insidious warmth that was even now spreading through her body at his nearness. Her only defence was to pretend it wasn't happening and hope her hormones would go back into hibernation some time soon.

The absolute worst, most shameful part was that she was pretty sure he knew exactly what his physical proximity did to her—she just hoped that he was so used to women going weak at the knees when he was around that he barely noticed any more.

She lifted her lashes to flash him another look through the dark mesh and found her eyes connecting with his. Her eyes grew wide for a moment before she dragged them away—no, those intent eyes of his noticed absolutely everything, she decided. It was the thoughts that might be going on behind their deep, dark surface that raised the question mark because, although she had the distinct impression he could read her like a book, she struggled to see past his mask.

'There's a knack to this,' she husked out as she bent to the task of unfastening the sleeping child's restraint, biting her lip as her trembling-fingered clumsiness contradicted her claim. Pushing her hair back impatiently—she had lost the velvet ribbon that had secured it at her nape at some point in the journey—she gritted her teeth, told herself to man up and completed the operation without waking Ellie.

'So you already said about the car seat,' he replied in the tone of a man who was not amused. 'But I'd like the chance to learn.'

'If she kicks off you'll be glad you're not carrying her. She can be pretty cranky when she's tired.'

The attempt at conciliation slid off Rio like sea water off a seal and his jaw clenched. He wasn't keeping count—actually, that wasn't true; he was. He remembered each and every time she'd rebuffed any attempt he made to help with Ellie. Once he might have put it down to Gwen's bloody-minded independence but that wasn't what this was about. When he went anywhere near the child she went straight into guard-dog mode.

'I'm fine with you not trusting me.'

*Except you're not, are you, Rio?*

Recognition of the fact flickered in his eyes before he half lowered his heavy lids and went on to incise with heavy irony, 'But I think even I've already grasped the basic concept that dropping a child is not a good idea.' *His* child that she would have kept from him her whole life so they'd have ended up as complete strangers to one another… Through sheer force of will he stopped feeding his anger, drawing a veil across the relentless stream of pointless *could have* scenarios, and instead heaved out a sigh and all the anger with it.

He could carry on being angry with Gwen but it wasn't going to move them on from this point if he wanted this child in his life. He had let the resentment go, even though at the moment that remained a goal rather than reality.

'It's got nothing to do with trust. Why do you have to make everything so personal?' she asked.

His ebony brows hit his equally dark hairline and his eyes slid to the face of the sleeping child before returning to Gwen's. 'She's my child—does it get more personal than that?'

Gwen hated the flush that she felt climb to her cheeks and hated him for making her feel guilty. 'Just how long are you going to punish me for? I only ask because children tend to pick up on tense atmospheres and—'

'So you want me to pretend that everything is sweetness and light between us?'

Her eyes flew wide in rejection as she ejaculated in utter revulsion, 'Oh, God, no!'

Her parents' life had been and presumably still was one long pretence, her mother pretending to believe her serial adulterer husband every single time he promised his latest fling was over and he'd never stray again. Her father pretending he had every intention of forsaking all others for his wife.

The only thing that seemed to unite her parents was a determination to maintain appearances, appear happy, pretending to be the perfect loving couple in front of their friends and neighbours.

Belatedly aware of Rio's speculative stare, she lowered her gaze and took a deep restorative breath. 'I intend to be honest with my daughter.'

'So what honest answer were you going to give her when she asked you who her father was?'

She glared at him in defiance.

'Or hadn't you thought that far ahead?'

The fight drained away, leaving her feeling weak and vulnerable and unable to think of any retort that sounded smarter than the truth.

'Sometimes I rarely think beyond the end of a day.'

'That's not an answer.'

She gave a weary sigh. 'Yes, I had thought about what I'd say to her and to be honest I…' Her voice cracked and she swallowed hard. 'I just know what I *wanted* to be able to tell her. I wanted to be able to tell her that her father loved her.' She compressed her quivering lips, her blue eyes lifting to his. 'Maybe now I can?'

Looking into her exhausted white face, he felt something twist hard inside his chest and looked away, unwilling to acknowledge the surge of emotion he hid behind a gruff response. 'You won't need to tell her anything now. I'll be there and she'll know it first-hand from me.'

As Gwen stared up at him the sudden hum of tension that had filled the air between them evaporated and he placed a guiding hand in the small of her back, leaving her unsure if she should interpret his words as a promise or a threat.

'This will save for another time. You look shattered. Just try and remember that the object of this exercise is for me to get to know my daughter, which you agreed was a good idea. But that is going to be kind of hard if you won't let me get within ten feet of her without going into "protective tiger mother" mode.'

*My daughter...* The possessive inflection in his voice dispelled the embryonic, uncomfortable stirrings of guilt she had been experiencing. 'I think *agreed* is overstating it, but obviously I'm fine with you holding her...' she lied with stiff, unfriendly formality.

He snorted and she blushed. 'I'm only thinking about Ellie.' She stopped as she recognised the untruth in her claim. It was her own life with him in it in *any* role that she was thinking of. She gave a tiny frustrated shake of her head and bent down to pick up Ellie. 'I'm just not used to—' She straightened up with a little grunt of effort that she had noticed was getting louder. She looked down at the sleeping toddler with her thumb in her mouth and gently settled her head on her shoulder to follow Rio off the plane towards yet another car, wondering how much longer she would be able to carry her daughter this way.

There was an ironic twist to the wistful half-smile that curved her lips. Gwen had smiled politely when people told her to enjoy these early years with her child because they flew by, but she hadn't really believed them—it was just something that people said. But she was starting to realise that they said it precisely because it was true. Those early months had already flown by but she still had precious memories to sustain her.

Rio had never had that time with Ellie, and he had no memories. The guilt came rushing back in a nauseating wave—anger was so much easier to bear.

It seemed like only yesterday that she had been wishing away these early years, dreaming of a day when Ellie was older and not needing the amount of childcare she required now. Being less hands-on would leave her with some time to herself. She would prefer not to identify the urge that had made her push Rio aside moments earlier as something perilously close to jealousy—she really didn't want to be that person!

Rio scanned her upturned features, watching the flow of emotions across her remarkably expressive face, and felt a strange twisting sensation in his chest that took him unawares.

Maybe it was the contrast between the tilt of her stubborn chin and the purple shadows beneath her incredible eyes that had dragged this unexpected—no, *unheard-of*—response from him.

Or maybe it was because he was closely examining her beautiful face with its soft, smooth skin and he could feel his libido pounding against the iron leash of his self-control. It was not something he normally had a problem with as his control over his emotions was always what had set him apart from his brother. But now it seemed as if the heat in the pit of his belly, the pounding of desire, was something he was going to have to learn to live with when he was around Gwen.

'I suppose I've got used to not relying on anyone,' she admitted and, despite his iron grip on himself, he flinched slightly.

# CHAPTER SEVEN

WITHIN SECONDS THE air between them was thick and thrumming with a different kind of tension this time… Their eyes remained connected, sealed, and Gwen couldn't have broken free if she had wanted to.

She didn't want to.

Did his molten hooded stare hold some sort of hidden message? She didn't know and she couldn't breathe as he seemed to be leaning into her. Her head lifted as his mouth lowered and she could see the tiny silvered flecks deep in his dark eyes and felt the equally dark thrum in her blood as her knees went weak. But then Ellie shifted in her arms and let out a whimper.

The spell was broken, the small cry shattering it like splintering ice, or maybe it had all been in her fevered imagination, Gwen mused, glad of the sweep of hair that hid her too warm cheeks, as she laid a soothing hand on her daughter's head before placing her gently in the car and getting in herself. Unfortunately there was nothing imaginary about the trickle of moisture pooling in the valley between her breasts and, despite the air-conditioned cool of the car, her clothes were sticking to her hot skin.

*Not magic, Gwen, just sex,* she told herself. The brutal truth hurt, but then so did discovering that fairy-tale happy endings only happened in, well, fairy tales. She was still feeling ashamed of that little rush of excitement that had left curls of heat in the pit of her belly when he spoke.

'I think you've already proved your point that you are Super Mum,' he said.

The smooth skin between her delicately delineated brows formed a tiny pleat. 'I...what do you mean? I'm not trying to be super anything.' She classed a good day as one when she didn't feel utterly inadequate. Her eyes flickered wider, suspicion settling in the cooling blue depths as she looked over at him as he drove fast with an effortless skill. 'Have you been asking people about me?' Looking for dirt, fuel for a highly paid lawyer who would paint her as a hopeless mother?

He rolled his eyes. 'Now don't go getting all paranoid on me again,' he drawled.

Her mouth opened. 'I'm not…' She closed it with a snap and a sigh before tacking on reluctantly, 'All right, maybe I am being a little suspicious, but have you been telling people that you're Ellie's father?'

'Would it be so terrible if I had?'

Gwen compressed her lips over a retort and reminded herself that it was always good to choose your battleground. This, she decided, looking around the confines of the car, wasn't it. Glancing out of the window, she realised that they had left the motorway behind them now and they hadn't passed a car for miles.

His jaw clenched as he met her combative blue stare. 'Relax.' It was advice that could have equally been directed at him as well, she thought, noting the tense muscles across his shoulders. 'I haven't said anything; you just came up in the conversation.'

Which told her absolutely nothing. She compressed her lips and glared at him. 'Conversation with who, exactly?'

'Being a VIP guest involves listening politely even when you're bored. The headmaster of your school spoke highly of you, as did the head of lower school, and before you go all conspiracy theory on me I didn't ask about you.' But Rio had listened rather than tune out what they'd been saying. 'It seems that among your colleagues it is an accepted fact that you have no flaws,' he said, eyes swivelling in the mirror to touch the curve of her neck where in the gathering darkness the skin there had an opalescent sheen that was indeed flawless.

The effort of dragging his attention away from her and back to the road added another groove to the frown lines between his brows.

No one he spoke to had mentioned that mouth of hers, though he was pretty sure several of them had noticed it. But they had stuck to less inflammatory subjects like her devotion as a parent and her incredible teaching skills.

'I don't appreciate the sarcasm.'

He cut off her protest with a disarming smile. 'Not even a little bit…?' He held a thumb and forefinger a whisper apart. 'Don't worry, I'm exceptionally subtle. I forgot your name twice to put them off the scent.'

She gave a snort. 'Sledgehammer-subtle.'

His mouth lifted in one corner in a half-smile. 'Why would it bother you when no one had a bad word to say about you?'

'Maybe you asked the wrong people.' Her parents would have told him what a disappointment she was to them—they told everyone else in their social circle. 'Some people think that having Ellie ruined my life.'

He arched a brow. 'What people?'

'My parents…or, at least, my father.' But then she shook her head, remembering how her mum had not defended her when her father had insisted she get rid of her precious baby.

Her nostrils quivered as she pushed the memories away, swallowing hard before she looked directly at Rio with defiance shining in her eyes. Her father had made her choose between them and her baby and it truly amazed Gwen that he had been shocked when she had told him she had every intention of keeping her baby.

'I'm not trying to steal her away from you, Gwen. I just want to share her.'

The quiet assertion took her breath away, and returned the shadow of wariness to her eyes, as once again his ability to read her thoughts and feelings was unsettling.

'I'm not afraid of you, Rio.' Perhaps she ought to be?

'But you don't trust me.'

It was a statement.

'You have Ellie's interests at heart and so do I—we are on the same team, and we need to work together,' he added.

'You sound so reasonable.' *Which obviously makes* me *the unreasonable one and in a moment I'll even be apologising*, she thought irritably.

'She isn't going to love you any less when new people come into her life.' He sensed her eyes were on his face but the road had narrowed at this point, as they joined the mountain track that led down to the beach house, and it took all his attention.

'Well, thank you for those words of wisdom, Professor. What sort of selfish, possessive, *needy* idiot do you think I am?' The car jolted and she grabbed for the door handle to steady herself.

'Sorry, we had the track resurfaced last year but there were some bad storms last winter.'

'How far is it?' she asked, clinging on as they jolted along.

'Not far now.'

'Is it a big resort?'

He flashed her a look before turning his eyes back to the road. 'Not a resort as such, just a beach house, and the mountain road meant that the area has remained totally undeveloped. My brother and I used to come here during the summer with our parents, and when they divorced she moved in and renovated it, pretty much rebuilt it.'

'So did they remarry other people, your parents?'

'My father died a few years ago.' There was *something* in his voice, but his expression gave away nothing of his feelings.

'Oh, I'm sorry to hear that.'

'We were not close.'

'And your mother? Did she—?'

'My mother is making up for lost time.'

'Lost time?'

'Her marriage to my father was not good at all. He was a jealous bastard who tried to manipulate and control every aspect of her life.'

'Oh!' It seemed a pretty inadequate response but Gwen couldn't think of what else to say.

'Right, here we are.' They were drawing into the courtyard, which surrounded the house on three sides.

'It's beautiful.'

'It looks even better in daylight and I can't take responsibility for the landscaping. The honour goes to an ancestor from a couple of centuries ago but my mother rediscovered the skeleton of the original garden lost under a lot of neglect, and she had it restored.' One of his earliest happy memories was of his mother wearing a straw hat on her head and holding a trowel in her hand, bossing around the gardeners.

As they came to a halt the lights came on, presumably activated by sensors, illuminating the low-lying stone building. One side of it, which overlooked the sea, seemed to be made entirely of glass, and the sea itself reflected a silver sheen off the dark shadows of the hills either side of the sheltered bay.

'It's beautiful.' His idea of a beach house was very different from her own!

'Yes, it is.'

'Not at all what I was expecting.'

'I will show you around once you have settled in.' He stepped out of the car and walked around to the passenger door, opening it for her.

She climbed out, enjoying the fact that the warmth was far less oppressive here than it had been in the airport. The light breeze smelt wonderfully of the sea and the wild thyme that grew between the cobbles underfoot.

She hesitated, half anticipating an army of staff to come running out to greet them.

'I hope you don't mind but for the first few days I thought it might be helpful for us to be alone here. I gave the staff some time off, though, if you prefer, I can recall them?'

She shook her head, some of the tension leaving her shoulders.

'The food is arranged, the kitchen is stocked with provisions, and there are meals already prepared in the freezer. Estelle is a very good cook, and she is also the housekeeper here. She supervised the arrangements before she left.'

'Arrangements?'

'The house has not seen children for a long time, not since—' His eyes wandered over the high stone wall to the right; he was clearly lost in memories.

'Since?' she prompted, wondering at an expression that was close to wistful that had drifted across his hard features.

He turned to look at her. 'Since I was a child. May I?' He tilted his head towards the sleeping child still in the car.

She nodded. 'Go ahead.'

She felt her throat tighten as she watched how carefully he bent and picked Ellie up, as though she might break. She grabbed the bag that contained the baby essentials that she had packed separately and followed him down the cobbled path and under an arch of clematis and honeysuckle.

'The pool,' he said, rather unnecessarily, indicating the infinity pool cut into the rock, which was surrounded by a terrace of flowers.

Ellie nestling on his shoulder like a baby animal, he punched numbers into a keypad and as if by magic the entire glass wall slid apart silently, the glass seeming to vanish inside the walls.

'Wow!'

'It's pretty much open-plan.' He pressed another button and the room was illuminated by recessed lights in the ceiling and tiled floor. The massive space stretched the entire width of the house, incorporating several seating areas with massive sofas, a long polished oak antique table that could have seated twenty, a grand piano that took pride of place one end, with bookshelves the other, and a modernistic wood burner hung suspended from the ceiling in the middle of the room.

She'd already said wow so she just stared.

'Kitchen is that way, study's off to that side and the bedrooms are in the other two wings.'

Gwen heard him but she was too busy staring at a corner of the room where there was a tall doll's house, several tubs of toys and a doll's pram.

'If they're not the right kind of toys, you can—'

'They're absolutely right. She'll love them all.'

'This is the nursery,' he said. There was a wooden child gate across the doorway and a faint smell of paint as they walked into a bright square room with a frieze of rabbits around the wall. The bed in the corner was painted to resemble a castle and there was a cot at the far end of the room.

'I wasn't sure if she needed a cot or a bed.'

Gwen looked at the bed with the safety sides, a little girl's dream. 'This looks perfect as she's already started trying to climb over the sides of her cot. Thank you, this is all very thoughtful.' A lot seemed to have been achieved in a short space of time.

She had thought it was impossible but Rio actually looked embarrassed.

'Your room adjoins this one, and there is just the small corridor that way. The child monitors are in every room and the volume control is on the pad by the door.'

He looked at the bed and hesitated. 'Shall I put her to bed?'

'Yes, please.' She took a deep breath and thought, *You've got to let go some time, Gwen.* 'I'll leave you to it, while I'll explore a bit if you don't mind.'

It was a gesture but a start and he seemed to recognise it as such. 'Thank you,' he said quietly.

Gwen made her way back to the car, popping her head around the door of the incredibly appointed modern kitchen on the way. They were clearly not going to be roughing it in any way!

At the car, she selected the bags that contained her essentials and some more stuff for Ellie and made her way back to the house. She was halfway there when she was intercepted by Rio.

'No, I'm fine.' Her fingers tightened around the handle of the heaviest bag.

Her stubborn determination to retain her grip brought her up against his chest and as his fingers curled over her own, it wasn't just the unexpected impact that made her gasp. She knew she should be doing something else rather than standing there panting, her small gasps now less to do with exertion and more to do with the buzz of expectation that tightened like a fist in her belly as the last remaining resistance drained from her body in one slow shuddering breath.

Gwen's eyes drifted closed, Rio's lean male body and the support of the hard breadth of his chest the only things keeping her standing. She was vaguely conscious of the bags hitting the floor but much more aware of his fingers pushing into her hair, his hand sliding to her waist and the words of husky Spanish as his hot breath stirred the skin of her cheek.

'I want you...'

*Did I just say that to him?*

She must have done because he was replying to her, but in Spanish, the words sounding as fevered as he felt. She leaned in at the waist, increasing the pressure of his erection against the softness of her belly. He was still murmuring against her mouth, her lips parted, willing the words to be lost in her mouth.

It took a couple of seconds for either of them to react to the sudden racket that cut through the still of the night. With a soft cry that was lost in the deafening sound of a helicopter flying incredibly low over their heads, Gwen sprang back, her hand pressed to her trembling mouth, her eyes wide and shocked.

Rio hadn't moved. He stood as still as a statue, Gwen's bags dragging around his feet, his face raised to the sky as he raked a hand through his dark hair. He let loose a string of fluent curses in several languages as he followed the helicopter lights above them with unfriendly eyes.

The noise diminished as the flashing lights moved farther away, remaining loud but no longer deafening.

Gwen was shaking like someone who had just stepped neck deep into a pool of ice water. 'Does that happen often?' she asked desperately, trying hard to sound normal, although it was incredibly difficult when her entire body was thrumming with frustration.

What was it about Rio that turned her into a totally different person, a person she barely recognised?

'No.'

'What's wrong?' *Beyond the fact you dissolved the moment he touched you,* she thought with dismay. There had been no gradual build-up—the passion had simply exploded between them and she was still shaking inside and out.

'We have a visitor.' He took his narrowed eyes off the distant lights where the helicopter had just put down. 'The only question is, is it my mother or my brother? I didn't expect either of them.'

The idea of meeting a member of his family at any time would have bothered her, but now, when her emotions felt so exposed and raw, and when all she wanted to do was… No, she didn't want to think about what she wanted to do right now. An interruption was a good thing, she insisted to herself.

*Delaying the inevitable, Gwen?*

Ignoring the goading voice in her head, she lifted her chin. 'You have a brother?'

Looking distracted, Rio nodded, a faint frown line pleating his brow as he gave her his attention. Or at least he looked at her mouth, as pink and swollen as though he had got as far as kissing her. 'Didn't I mention him before?'

'There's no reason you should have, is there? I should go inside and check that the noise didn't wake Ellie.'

'Fine. You do that and I'll go and check out the visitor.' He half turned, then paused. 'Don't worry, they won't be staying.'

'You can't make them go!' she exclaimed in shock.

He flashed a white grin. 'Oh, I can be very persuasive.'

Didn't she already know it!

Not that his persuasive powers were all that tested where she was concerned. Because all he had to do was touch her and she was lost. 'But what will you—?'

Her words were addressed to thin air as he had gone, his long legs quickly distancing him from her until the dark swallowed him up, leaving her wondering what the hell was about to happen. What was he going to tell their unexpected visitor?

With a deep sigh and a last resentful glare into the darkness, Gwen made her way to the nursery, where Ellie, oblivious to everything going on, was still sound asleep. Gwen had no excuse to linger in the nursery although she was tempted because, despite Rio's very inhospitable stance, she couldn't imagine that their visitor would not be staying the night at the very least. Of the two possibilities, she would have preferred it to be Rio's brother who had arrived. He might be less judgemental about Ellie and was less likely to view her with the maternal suspicion she felt sure his mother would.

Gwen made her way back to the sitting room and sat down on the piano stool. She was still sitting there five minutes later when Rio returned, pushing a wheelchair.

Feeling like a guilty schoolgirl caught some place she wasn't allowed, Gwen shot to her feet, but her apprehension dissolved as she met the smiling and teary eyes of the woman sitting in it.

Despite the chair and the plaster leg extended before her, this wasn't a frail figure. This slim woman, her dark hair flecked with silver, instead projected an air of vitality despite her confinement and certainly did not look old enough to be a grown man's mother. The mother of *two* grown men, she silently corrected.

Lady Cavendish extended her hands and without thinking about it Gwen found herself walking towards her, her own hands held out until they were enfolded in the cool grasp of the elegant older woman.

'My dear girl, firstly I must apologise. I came looking for one son and found the other.' Her head turned towards Rio. 'And not just a son but a granddaughter too.' Her voice thickened with emotion. 'I can't tell you how happy I am and I know you will forgive me for intruding like this.' She threw her son another look, this one satirical. 'Even though Rio will not ask you, but…could I see her? For just a moment or two? Oh, I promise that I won't wake her. But just to *see* her…' She swallowed, visibly moved by the prospect. 'My grandchild.'

Gwen felt herself relaxing and responded to the charm and appeal in those lovely velvety eyes without thinking.

'Of course you can,' she said warmly, contrasting this stranger's reaction to becoming a grandparent to that of her own parents.

'And then I will be gone. You won't even know I've been here and I'll only be a moment, I promise.'

She was actually five minutes, and when she and Rio returned there was evidence of more tears on her cheeks along with a few streaks of mascara.

'She is very beautiful. You must be so proud of her.'

Gwen nodded. 'She looks like Rio,' she said, and immediately felt embarrassed, not because it was a lie, but because *he* was beautiful too and a few minutes earlier she had wanted to touch and love every beautiful inch of him. Now she was talking to his mother, whose eyes were enough like Rio's to make her wonder if she could also read her mind.

'Yes, he and Roman were beautiful babies too.'

Standing behind the wheelchair, Rio said something that sounded impatient in Spanish.

'Yes, Rio, I am just going—but am I allowed to ask for a glass of water first?'

'Because there is no water on board?'

'Because I need to take my painkillers.'

The quirk of Rio's lips was immediately replaced by a downward tug of concern. He said something in Spanish and vanished.

'Are you in pain? Can I do anything?'

'Oh, heavens, no, it's only a little discomfort and I'm rather frustrated because I thought

I'd be up and around by now…but things are not healing as they ought. I'm booked in for surgery, a new pin and…but enough of that. No, I'm actually not in any significant pain, it was just a little ruse to get rid of Rio for one moment so that I could talk to you in private.'

'This must have been a shock for you,' Gwen said, feeling her way cautiously. It would be a lot easier to navigate this conversation if she had a clue what Rio had already told his mother about them.

'A marvellous surprise! I never thought I'd ever have a grandchild. My sons…can I be frank with you?' Without waiting for a response, she pushed on, speaking quickly. 'Well, I don't know how much you know, but my own marriage was not a good one, and while we were together my boys were my champions. They should not have needed to be and the knowledge shames me greatly. I am afraid that witnessing my marriage has left scars for them both. Not the kind of scars you can see,' she added, glancing at her own leg. 'Though in the past I always knew that at least then they had each other to lean on. But now one is…' Her smile suddenly flashed out, soothing away the lines of worry on her face.

'But no matter,' she husked, brushing away an emotional tear from her cheek. 'Rio has you and Ellie now.'

Gwen realised with dawning horror that Rio's mother had got the totally wrong idea about them. 'Rio and I, we are not really—'

'Oh, I realise that you have been apart for a while. The whys of that are not my business, although if ever you need to talk about anything, I am here. But it's not the past that matters, it's the *now* that is most important. Rio has moved on, he has found happiness, which makes me so very happy. He has been so lonely, I think.'

Gwen kept her expression neutral as she thought about the countless covetous female eyes that followed Rio whenever he walked into a room. If his mother thought he led the life of a lonely monk, it was not for Gwen to disillusion her.

'The boys were so young when the responsibility of the business fell on their shoulders, and then when Roman walked away and left it all for Rio to manage, it must have been very hard. But he has never complained, you know, and he never did. He was such a *loving* little boy.'

Rio a little boy…a *loving* little boy! The images planted in her head by the poignant words made Gwen's chest tighten.

'And so spontaneous, before he sadly became so closed off… Their father used to pump them about me for information. What I was doing, who I was doing it with, if you get my drift?'

Gwen, who did and was horrified, nodded. The story explained a lot of things about Rio and her tender heart ached for him.

'There was one occasion when Rio blurted something out the way boys do in excitement and his father used the information to…' She shook her head sadly, not completing the sentence. 'From being spontaneous Rio became very self-contained—they both did, which was all right while they had each other. So, you see, that is why I am so glad Rio has his own family now.'

Gwen felt a wave of helplessness. She simply didn't have it in her to wipe the glow of happiness from this lovely woman's beautiful

face by telling her the truth about her relationship with Rio.

An image of Rio watching Ellie sleep flashed
into her head. 'I think he'll be a good father,'
she said, and found herself meaning it.

'Your glass of water, Mother?'

Gwen jumped guiltily and turned to see
Rio standing there. How much had he heard,
if anything? His expression told her nothing. It seemed that the lessons he'd learnt as a
child had been perfected during the interven-
ing years. There was very little in his face of
the young boy who'd blurted out the wrong
thing to his father about his mother and then
blamed himself for it. This was the man who,
it seemed, shouldered his brother's burdens
along with his own with no complaints and,
as far as she could see, with no expectation
of thanks.

'Oh, I managed to swallow the pills without
water,' she said airily. 'It has been so nice to
meet you, Gwen.' She raised a cheek, a gesture that Gwen correctly interpreted, bending
to awkwardly kiss her.

'And you, Lady Caven—'

'Call me Jo—everyone does—and I hope to see you all very soon.'

Gwen followed mother and son outside and sat down on a bench on the terrace. She was still sitting there in the warm darkness when she heard the crunch of gravel heralding Rio's return.

'Is your brother missing?' she asked as Rio came within her line of sight. 'Is that why your mother was looking for him?'

Rio dug his hands into the pockets of the well-cut trousers that were moulded to his powerful thighs. 'Not missing, just off the grid for a while like me.'

'Your mother seems worried about you both.'

'It goes with the job of being a mother, you should know that. But Roman is a grown man, and is well able to take care of himself.'

'So you're not concerned about him at all?'

'I am not.'

It wasn't concern she could read in his expression, but there was definitely something—something to do with a falling-out between the brothers his mother had alluded to…

'What did you tell your mother about Ellie and me? She seems to think we're a family now.'

'I told her the truth, or a partial version of it, and it really doesn't matter what she thinks, does it? It doesn't matter what anyone thinks. This is about us and what *we* think.'

The reference to *us* gave her a little warm glow. It answered an unacknowledged need in her to belong, something she'd never really had before.

'Earlier...' she began awkwardly.

He took a step towards her and she got to her feet swiftly, her hand raised in silent protest. 'It's all too much, too soon, Rio. I need to think.'

A muscle in Rio's jaw clenched and he let out a slow breath.

'Thinking can be overrated, but fine.' His eyes moved across her face, the hunger in them morphing into something gentler as he noted the dark shadows under her eyes. 'You must be tired.'

'It has been a long day. I haven't even the faintest idea what the time is.'

'Ten-thirty.' He hesitated. 'Would you like some supper?'

'No, I had some sandwiches on the plane. I'm not hungry and, to be honest, I wouldn't mind turning in.'

'Of course.' He tipped his head. 'Goodnight, Gwen.'

She held her breath as he leaned forward but the kiss never came. He just brushed aside a strand of hair that had fallen in her eyes before he straightened up. There was nothing even vaguely erotic about his action but she was trembling as she walked towards the house, too ashamed to respond to his soft goodnight.

# CHAPTER EIGHT

AFTER TWO HOURS of trying to bury the fact that the smell of Gwen's hair had aroused him to the point that even ten minutes of standing in a cold shower didn't work, Rio gave up trying to sleep. It wouldn't be buried and his ache just wouldn't go away.

In the end, he grabbed a pair of shorts and walked out into the warm, humid night. Ignoring the pool, he headed for the beach; he knew the tides quite well and felt safe swimming in the sea.

The repetitive action of swimming up and down eventually had the soothing mind-and-body-numbing result he had hoped for. He had forgotten to take a towel but the walk over to the house dried the moisture off his skin and he was dragging his hands through his sable hair to remove the excess water as he approached the house. He took the shorter route that cut past the pool, its turquoise depths still lit by the solar-powered underwater lights.

He was almost tempted to swim again but his body had achieved a level of relaxation that might enable him to actually get some sleep.

He was about to turn back to the house when he saw her, and all the benefits of thirty minutes of open-sea swimming vanished in a heartbeat.

Wearing a silky-looking cream nightshirt, Gwen was standing on the edge of the pool balanced on one foot, her other extended so her toes were dangling in the water. Presumably she hadn't been able to sleep either, maybe for the same reason he couldn't?

The possibility sent a fresh pulse of raw desire through his body.

She looked up suddenly as if she sensed his presence and he instinctively pulled back into the shadow of the overhanging trees but then stopped himself. It felt too voyeuristic to watch her when she didn't know he was there.

He swallowed and stepped forward instead. 'Are you thinking of swimming?'

'No, I'm just looking.' Gwen couldn't stop *looking* and there was nothing *just* about it!

Rio looked like a bronze god walking towards her, all rippling muscles and golden skin. He looked primitive, the very essence of maleness, his every move displaying a grace and raw strength that was simply mind-blowing. Anticipation made her heart thud, her legs were shaking… She was shaking all over, in fact.

He stopped a couple of feet away from her and by this point she could barely breathe, let alone think. She was simply suffocated by lust; her skin prickled with it, drawing the nipples of her round breasts into taut, tingling peaks. She wasn't in the water but she felt as though she were drowning.

'This would be crazy.' Her voice sounded as if it belonged to someone else.

A nerve clenched in his cheek. 'I don't care.'

She was shaking with excitement and as her passion-glazed eyes connected with his, the blatant sensuality of his stare sent a heavy throb of need through her body.

She gave a smile that sparkled with reckless energy. 'Neither do I.' Holding his eyes, she took the hem of the nightshirt she wore and pulled it over her head, tossing it away, oblivious to the fact it landed in the pool.

Watching through a haze of desire, he groaned and lunged, not in any specific order. One muscular arm banded around her ribs, the other behind her head as he lifted her until their faces were level.

Her lips parted eagerly under the pressure of his mouth, inviting the sensual invasion of his plunging tongue, and as he tasted her she felt as though he would drain her.

He lifted his head and she could see there were dark stripes of colour along the crests of his cheekbones. 'Trust me.'

'I do.' Crazily it was true.

He skimmed his tongue over the surface of her lips. 'I want to see you lose control,' he slurred against her lips.

She whimpered and panted as he put her down and slid down her body, his hands on her breasts while his mouth traced a path between them. The muscles of her belly quivered as he slid even lower, then as her legs gave way he pulled her down to join him, rolling her underneath him, pausing only to remove his shorts.

His hands were pressed against hers stretched

high above her head as he kissed her, his hips moving against her soft belly, letting her feel the strength of his arousal as his erection grazed her stomach. But it only made her more frantic to feel him properly, with all of him inside her.

'Did I say that out loud?' she wondered.

He lifted his face from where it was pressed into her neck. 'You shouted it. Call me *cariad* again.'

'*Cariad...*' she whispered obediently even though she didn't know she'd already said the Welsh endearment once. Her eyes drifted closed as the mixture of sensations was just too much to absorb. The long, hot, drugging kisses were draining her of any remaining strength of will and they were just making her ache for even more.

'I want to touch you,' she gasped.

He groaned, his face contorted with an agonised expression. 'Later... Now I just need...'

'Oh, God...' she panted, and widened her legs as she felt him begin to enter her. 'Yes, please, Rio!'

She arched her back, losing every vestige of self-control as she cried out his name again, urging him on as he filled her full of him, absorbing the powerful, driving thrusts that aroused every nerve ending and pushed her towards a climax that wrenched a wild, raw cry from her throat.

He lay there panting on top of her while Gwen slowly floated back to reality, which was that she was lying on a cold, hard tiled surface. Until now she had not even registered the discomfort.

'Let's use a bed next time,' he whispered in her ear as he rolled off her.

'Is there to be a next time?' she teased lightly, kissing the palm of the hand that was still thrown across her chest.

His dark eyes glittered wickedly down at her as he raised himself up on one elbow. 'You know that I always rise to a challenge.'

Gwen resisted the tug that brought her surfacing from sleep, her reluctance finally overcome by curiosity, the feeling that something was *different*. And then it all came back with a rush that made her suck in a short shocked breath as a stream of images and sensations began to flow through her head.

Without opening her eyes, she now knew that the weight she felt across her waist was Rio's arm thrown across it and the warmth was his long hair-dusted legs that were tangled with her own.

She didn't analyse the sense of rightness or safety that it gave her. Who wouldn't feel right waking up entangled with a man who looked, felt and made love like Rio?

She lay there enjoying the moment. She had finally fallen asleep in the early hours with her head on his chest. It was still there now, and the sound she was listening to was the soft, slow boom of his heartbeat.

She remembered him asking did she want him to go back to his own bed.

She must have said no, but she didn't recall doing so.

She lay still, willing herself to absorb every detail, each impression, knowing she would want to relive this moment in her head later. She wanted to remember the feel of all the little whorls of chest hair that tickled her chin, the musk of his warm skin, the weight of his arm, and the way his fingers curved across the angle of her hip.

She wanted the moment to last for ever, but of course it wasn't going to. Her brain was not content with staying in neutral and her thoughts were already racing around like a frantic hamster on a wheel.

As the thoughts crowded in she couldn't lie still any longer. Holding her breath, she carefully pressed a hand into the mattress and eased her weight back, sliding out from underneath his arm. Balanced on the edge of the bed now, with just his thigh holding her there, she lifted her head and angled it to take a look at his face.

From this position she could see the perfect carved contours of his face, the angles and hollows emphasised by a night's worth of dark stubble, his long eyelashes lying dark against the perfect slashing angle of his cheekbones.

The ache of longing inside her as she gazed at him was frightening in its intensity. Lifting a hand to blot away the tears she felt on her cheeks, she eased herself carefully away from the confining weight of his hair-roughened thigh, hating to break the contact with his warm body and shatter the lingering remnants of intimacy.

There was a very good reason Gwen hadn't allowed herself last night to think about what the morning would bring, and this aching hollow feeling in her stomach was it. Last night she had given herself over entirely to need, and she had accepted the *desperation* that had risen from the deepest part of her when he had touched her, not fought or questioned it.

This morning it wasn't the questions she was pushing away, it was the answers!

She reached down and picked up the gown she had folded across the end of the bed, which was now on the floor. Fighting her way silently into it, she tightened the belt and, without allowing herself a glance backwards, crept quietly along the small corridor that linked her room with Ellie's nursery.

She didn't go inside, just looked over the safety gate. This room was darker because of the blackout blinds behind the brightly patterned curtains. It took Gwen's eyes a few moments to adjust to the light cast by the two nightlights that projected a starry pattern on the ceiling and make out the dark curls above the low safety sides of the brightly painted castle bed.

Gwen could hear the soft sound of even baby breathing, and for a moment love banished the shadows lurking in her eyes. Did all mothers dream of the future they wanted their child to have, a future without any tears? Had her mother held her and thought that same way?

The guilt came as it always did, rational or not, whenever she thought of her own mother. Her sadness, the sense of betrayal she felt at her mother's actions, was always tinged with guilt.

Of course she knew that her mother could have walked away from her husband, but had *chosen* to stay, just as she had chosen not to defend her daughter, and that hurt the most. But despite everything Gwen couldn't shake the feeling that she had deserted her mam; she had chosen her baby over her mother.

She was momentarily tempted to go into the room and hold Ellie, breathe in all the warm, comforting, wholesome sweetness of her, but practicality won out. So instead of risking disturbing her daughter she stayed there a moment, just listening, before finally dragging herself away. Her bare feet were silent on the cool tiled surface as she turned and made her way into the massive light-filled living room. She touched a handle and one of the full-height sliding glass panels that made the outside and inside blend seamlessly together swished open silently. Gwen slipped through and into the dusky pre-dawn light.

She paused, breathing in the rich scents that filled the air that was already pleasantly warm before making her way through the garden that seemed to be planted with sensory appreciation in mind. Her robe brushed the sweet-smelling Mediterranean herbs, sending even more intense aromas into the air.

Without any real plan Gwen found herself skirting the pool, the memories of what they had shared there still too shockingly fresh. She felt like a different person when she was with Rio, a person she barely recognised.

By the time she'd walked down the broad steps onto the beach the sun was just rising over the horizon, spilling fingers of scarlet and gold out into the layered smoky grey and blue of the clear dawn sky.

Sinking ankle deep into the soft sand, she watched as the grey turned to bands of contrasting shades of blue split by red-gold that turned the sea a delicate shade of pale copper.

She felt her mood lift. It was hard not to feel hope in the face of nature's beauty, but her hope was tinged with confusion as the cool morning air washed away the last shreds of sleepiness and the light breeze blowing in off the water tugged at her hair. Gwen closed her eyes and lifted her chin, letting the breeze blow the heavy strands back from her face while the floor-length robe she had pulled on flapped against her bare legs.

There was nothing to hear but her heartbeat and the soft swishing murmur of the waves as they hit the white sand. The utter peace and serenity of her surroundings contrasted dramatically with her internal chaos of churning emotion.

The truth was meant to set you free, wasn't it?

She opened her eyes and gave a tiny self-mocking laugh that floated away on the breeze. Truth was overrated, especially when the truth of her feelings for Rio was simply tearing her apart.

Or was it *denying* them that was doing that?

asked the voice in her head. She shoved the question away, convinced it had more to do with self-preservation than rationality. That if she gave those feelings a name it would give them a power over her.

Last night they had made love...no, not made love, *had sex*, she reminded herself. Truth, she decided, wiping away a silent tear that was tracing a salty path down her cheek, was *definitely* overrated.

The tide had started to turn while she stood there and she jumped backwards as the water washed over her feet. She supposed she ought to go back. Ellie might wake soon and Rio... Would he wake and miss her or would he be relieved she'd left the bed to avoid the awkwardness of any morning-after pillow talk?

Perhaps he wouldn't feel awkward at all? Perhaps last night meant nothing to him except as a temporary convenience, because they were both there, available and willing? She threw up her hands and turned her back on the sea. God, when had life got so complicated?

*Since you fell—*

She choked off the thought, strangling it before it formed as she stormed up the beach.

The spurt of temper had only got her as far as the steps when she stopped.

Before she saw Rio she needed to decide how she was going to play this. How did he feel about last night?

Did she want last night to happen again?

Her white teeth ground together as a wave of disgusted impatience with herself washed over her. Why was she even asking these questions when she already knew the answers? Rio had not made it a secret in the past that all he wanted from any woman was no-obligation sex. He didn't do exclusivity or long term, and he didn't want permanent ties, but fate had introduced a game-changer to his life in the shape of Ellie who, against all the odds, he was clearly already madly in love with.

The only thing Rio was committed to was being a father to his new-found daughter. It would be dangerous for her to assume anything else had fundamentally changed between them.

The question remained—did she want last night to happen again, knowing that for him it had been as basic and uncomplicated as simply satisfying a carnal thirst?

No, she didn't want it, but, God, she *needed* it. She was still wearing the memory of last night's lovemaking like a second skin. It felt like a dream but the ache in several parts of her body told her it was all too real. A deep shudder ran through her at the skin-peeling intensity of it, the sheer overwhelming pleasure that had made her feel she was about to lose consciousness.

Without her realising, her steps had taken her right up to the beach house, which in the sunshine was now lit up by the golden light bouncing off the expanse of glass. She blinked in confusion. She still hadn't decided what she was going to do. She supposed she had to ask herself what price she was willing to pay for the exquisite pleasure of being back in his bed, albeit temporarily.

He'd share his body but was that enough for her? Did she even want what he would only ever give grudgingly, which was a deeper connection between them? He would no doubt say that they were now and always connected by their child, but Gwen wanted more than that and only a fool would fall for a man who was incapable of giving anything of himself beyond his body.

She had always sworn that she would never settle for a man who could give her any less than everything. She wanted love, and she wanted to be in a man's heart, not just his bed, but she also wanted Rio. Because she already *loved* him.

She was a fool.

'This is impossible!' she yelled loudly enough to drown out her own thoughts, and luckily there was no one to hear her other than the gulls drifting on warm air streams above her head.

She squeezed her eyes tight shut and clenched her hands, wishing with all her might that she could look at Rio and not feel so damned… *needy*!

Her eyes flew wide as a noise from inside the main living room, loud enough to penetrate the closed door, made her start, a noise that was the unmistakable sound of breaking glass.

Responding to a protective instinct deeply embedded inside her, Gwen was already moving, her first thought inevitably to check on Ellie. Even though logic told her that her daughter was safely tucked up in bed, even though she knew she'd turned up the volume on the monitor beside her bed so high that it would have woken someone in a coma, let alone a sleeping Rio!

In a few breathless seconds she had flung open the silent sliding doors and stepped inside. Her panic receded, the thud of her heartbeat slowing, when she spotted the cause of the noise. Shards of a tall cylindrical, dramatically hand-painted glass vase that had sat on a lamp table to the right of the grand piano were now scattered across the terracotta-tiled floor.

His broad back to her, Rio was bent over picking them up, swearing fluently in Spanish as he did so and paying scant regard to the fact that they looked razor sharp.

'Be careful,' she warned, alarm sharpening her tone. 'You'll cut yourself.'

At the sound of her voice Rio straightened rapidly and spun around, several shards of glass in one long-fingered hand. He looked struck dumb by the sight of her standing there. For once he was the one acting thrown by her presence, though displaying more shock than the situation warranted, it seemed to Gwen.

A frown flickered into her blue eyes as his dark stare swept upwards from her feet. She couldn't put her finger on it but he was acting very strangely. Perhaps his behaviour was linked with the previous night? Was he regretting it already?

The thoughts were flitting through her head when their eyes finally connected. The hand she had slid into her heavy chestnut hair to pull it back from her face fell down by her side.

She had unconsciously steeled herself for an emotional explosion, tensed in preparation of containing her usual reaction to him. The anticlimax was extreme: there was no explosion, no charge in the air between them, just air.

She felt… Actually she felt nothing at all. Her pulses were not leaping, there were no butterflies running riot in her stomach and no warm feeling in the pit of her stomach.

She felt…not needy!

Her first thought was that her prayers had been answered, her second was that there looked like a lot more than one night's stubble on his chin and under the stubble he looked paler than usual.

'Too late, I already have.' He extended his hand towards her, letting the blood drip unchecked from his thumb onto the white grand piano, before he blotted his hand against his trousers and then, as an afterthought, smeared the red blob off the piano with his sleeve.

Gwen, who was less indifferent to blood than he appeared to be, felt her stomach muscles quiver in sympathy with the injury.

His grimace implied indifference as he proceeded to rub his hand against his shirt, leaving a bloody smear to match the one on the piano before giving up with a shrug. 'Never mind. I'm sure Estelle will clean away the evidence.'

'She's not here.'

Gwen didn't add, *You sent everyone away so you could have some time getting to know your daughter before you shared the news with the world*, because at some point over the last few moments she had realised that she was talking, not to Rio, but to his brother. And not just any brother, but his *twin*.

His *identical* twin.

Rio's twin—Roman, wasn't it?—tilted his head to one side and for a moment looked less like Rio. In a similar situation Rio would have scrunched his forehead and—

'So who are you?'

Gwen discovered that her scrutiny was being returned by a very curious pair of familiar dark eyes, the difference being that in his gaze there was nothing even vaguely sexual or challenging or a thousand other things Rio managed to communicate to her with just one look.

She found herself gathering her robe a little tighter around her, feeling awkward. She felt many things when she was with Rio but awkward was not one of them.

There hadn't been time for Rio to contact his brother so this had to be a coincidence.

'I'm Gwen,' she said, even though she knew he would probably be none the wiser. 'You're Roman?'

'Hello, Gwen.' He gave a grin that was almost but not quite the same as Rio's. She noticed for the first time that he looked tired, and maybe she was being fanciful but to her it seemed there was a darkness, a sombreness behind his eyes that Rio didn't have.

Maybe she'd finally got used to being able to read Rio's expressions, or maybe she could just see clearer when she wasn't being blinded by the mad impulse to throw herself at his beautiful mouth like a suicidal rabbit when she saw a fox, which was something of a relief.

Her light musical trill of self-mocking laughter made Roman's eyebrows lift, which made her laugh again and think, *Just like Rio.*

There had to be at least half a dozen PhDs in it for the academics. Two men, so identical to look at, and while one had awoken a deep primal passion in her that she hadn't known she possessed, the other was just an *extremely* good-looking man who physically left her completely cold. It really was inexplicable.

'You actually *are* identical.' The moment the words were out of her mouth she felt foolish. How many times must he and Rio have heard that line? Luckily he was too polite to comment on her lack of originality, but she was sure that Rio wouldn't have shown a similar restraint.

'So people tell us, *Gwen*…?'

She nodded. 'Meredith.'

'Meredith or Gwen?' She knew Rio would

have accompanied the question with a mocking gleam in his eyes, but his brother didn't.

His brother seemed a more *intense* sort of person, this man who'd walked away from power and responsibility leaving Rio to shoulder the entire burden of their inheritance. It spoke of a certain selfishness to leave your brother holding the baby—though not that baby. Roman didn't know about Ellie yet.

Or did he?

Did they tell each other everything?

She knew that often twins were closer than ordinary siblings; some even claimed to have a telepathic connection—if one stubbed their toe, the other felt it.

Was that just an urban myth? She sincerely hoped so!

'My name is Gwen Meredith.'

'Are you Welsh?'

She nodded. 'I'm impressed. Not many people outside the UK would get the accent first time.'

'I'm the intuitive one, or so they say.'

Gwen, who had always found Rio uniquely intuitive, lowered her gaze rather than challenge his claim. It crossed her mind that perhaps people assigned twins' roles early on in childhood—bright twin, athletic twin, leader, follower, and so on—and they stuck to them unquestioningly throughout their whole lives.

She lifted her gaze and caught him yawning. He intercepted her look and grinned. 'Long drive, a last-minute decision to come. I thought I'd be here for the party. And you are staying here with…?' One dark brow floated upwards the same way she had noticed in Rio a hundred times, the likenesses as much as the differences between them fascinating Gwen. 'I am assuming that Rio is here?'

'He's in bed,' she blurted, then compounded her embarrassment by blushing like a teenager. 'That is… I mean…'

Rio's twin smiled wickedly and again Gwen was struck by the similarity of their posture and body language. 'I get the picture.'

She wanted to say, *No, you really don't because I hardly get it myself,* but stopped herself because he probably did, just not the entire picture! Still playing catch-up, she suddenly registered his earlier comment. *Party?*

What party did he mean?

'You should put something on that,' she said,

changing the subject as she nodded to indicate his finger that appeared to be still oozing blood, though to her relief it was no longer dripping. Rio would be oozing blood too, she decided, if he had deliberately kept her in the dark about some sort of party. The idea that Rio was manipulating her for some reason brought a spark of caution to her blue eyes.

'I'll live.' She sensed Roman had to put some effort into his smile. 'Look, I'm sorry if my arrival is badly timed but I'm off to my bed. I'll look in on Rio first, so could you point me in the direction of my big brother's...usual room?' He was already moving towards the door and Gwen was still nailed to the spot; similarly her tongue felt glued to the roof of her mouth.

'No...yes... I think maybe...your mother was looking for you earlier,' she stammered.

His brow knitted. 'She *was*? She left?'

Gwen nodded.

'So you have already met our mother?' There was a new interest in his eyes now as he studied her. 'Rio finally fetched a girl home!' He gave a low laugh, amused by his private joke.

Before she could figure out how to respond

to this the door to the hallway was pushed open, clearly with a foot, as that came into the room first, followed by a sleep-dishevelled Rio with a very wide-awake Ellie in his arms.

## CHAPTER NINE

IF ROMAN HAD looked surprised when he'd first seen Gwen, he now looked like a man who had put chocolate in his mouth and tasted hot chilli instead. He genuinely looked as though he could not believe his eyes as his astonished stare went from his bare-footed brother to the child he was carrying.

If he was even half as quick on the uptake as Rio it would take him only about a heart-beat to fill in the blanks.

Rio saw Gwen and felt a sense of relief that could not entirely be put down to the fact he felt somewhat out of his depth entertaining a very unpredictable toddler whose speech patterns remained a bit of a mystery to him. Understanding what she said was pretty much ninety per cent guesswork on his part and his mistakes elicited a bad-tempered response in his daughter, who, he was learning, got even louder when she was frustrated.

The communication problem was a two-way thing. She didn't appear to understand his requests, or maybe she just thought it was fine to ignore him—like mother, like daughter. The irony was that when he'd finally resorted to speaking Spanish out of sheer frustration, she seemed to respond to it just as well as his English!

He couldn't decide if it was the novelty value or the proof that children mopped up new languages like little sponges at this age, but they had got there in the end after a fashion. When he'd recalled his lack of empathy and patience when Gwen had been packing up to leave the cottage he'd felt a twinge of guilt—it seemed there was nothing like a two-year-old to teach a man some humility.

Getting a child out of bed, picking her up and coaxing her to stop crying was a lot less straightforward than it had first appeared. People really did downplay the difficulty of this parenting role! In his career there had been moments when he had felt a degree of complacent self-satisfaction when he'd pulled off a major financial deal against the odds and despite the critics, but that emotion paled beside the glow of triumph when they had gone in search of Gwen to show her how well they'd managed by themselves.

'So there you are. I should warn you to speak up, Gwen—I might have lost my hearing.' The child's cries, amplified by the volume control beside the bed, had woken him, but even that sound had been drowned out for a few moments when he'd realised Gwen was gone. Panic wasn't the right word, nor even a feeling of loss, he mused, his expression sobering as he remembered reaching out to feel a cold sheet that still bore the imprint of her body instead of soft warm skin.

His eyes drifted over the shape and warmness he had missed earlier. The robe she wore outlined the fluid grace of the lovely long lines of her body, her vibrant glowing hair lying loose and wild down her back, making him think of how it had felt as he'd trickled it through his fingers last night before burying his face in it.

'Where did you get to? Couldn't you sleep?' His voice slid a few husky notes lower. 'You really should have woken me.'

She had definitely slept for some of last

night at least. He knew that because he had lain awake himself for a while, just watching her gently breathing.

Her eyes were not closed now. They were urgently signalling some sort of message to him, but Ellie's curly head kept bobbing into his line of vision. He tilted his head to see around her and Ellie immediately yelled again, not wanting to be ignored.

Gwen stood there, silently discounting the twin telepathy theory. Rio clearly hadn't caught on to the fact that his brother was standing right behind him, but then he did have his hands full quite literally and she knew from experience that containing a wriggling Ellie took all your focus and strength, not to mention dexterity.

'Rio?' Gwen said, but the rest of her words were drowned out by an extra loud yell of complaint from Ellie. Rio went to put her down, probably thinking she wanted to run to her mother.

Gwen flung an arm out. 'Don't put her down yet, Rio. There's broken glass all over the floor!'

Rio swung her back up. *'Vamos en la piscina mas tarde—perfecto!'*

To Gwen's utter amazement Ellie stopped dead and looked at him.

'What did you say?'

'I said we'd go to the pool later.'

'She understood you?'

He shrugged and grinned. 'She is already fluent.'

She lost her fight not to respond to his grin. 'Will you be careful of the glass too?'

Rio was barefoot, but at some point since she'd left him he had pulled on a tee shirt and boxers. His hair was sticking up in sexy spikes, which probably had less to do with nature than with Ellie, looking equally tousled but very cute in a pair of rabbit pyjamas, who was now running strands of her father's dark hair through both chubby hands.

'Where were you, Gwen? We both missed you, didn't we, my sweetest?' Rio crooned, bending his head towards the toddler, who grabbed another handful of the thick, glossy hair that seemed to fascinate her. 'Ah...please don't give her scissors... Hmmm, yes, thank you, Ellie—I think that's what she's saying?'

The warmth in his eyes as they lifted and connected with her own would have melted Gwen like ice cream on a hot day in any other circumstances.

'What do you fancy for—?' He broke off, a frown forming between his brows as he scanned her face, apparently seeing something there that bothered him. 'Do we need to talk?'

Roman, who had coped with the sudden appearance of a woman wearing very little, but who was coping less well with his ruffled brother carrying a child who bore a really startling resemblance to him, finally recovered his voice.

'I think maybe we do,' Roman mused.

Hugging a squirming Ellie, who had finally got bored playing with his hair, a little closer, Rio turned jerkily to where his brother stood.

'*Roman...?* What—?' The rest of his rapid staccato response was delivered in Spanish.

Roman patiently waited his twin out, watching the child in his brother's arms with a fascinated eye as he replied, 'I knew you'd be glad to see me.'

Rio ignored the irony. 'Of course I'm glad to see you,' he lied. 'But I—'

Reading the appeal in his eyes as he turned to her, Gwen moved forward, holding out her arms to receive Ellie, who cried shrilly in protest and held out her arms demandingly to Rio.

'I'll just leave you two to it, shall I?' Gwen said, not waiting for a response as she headed for the door.

'You don't have to go, Gwen.' Rio simultaneously registered his twin's expression of surprise and the revealing flicker of pleasure on Gwen's face as he spoke.

He also recognised it was impractical for her to stay, as the things he needed to say to his brother would be hard enough without an audience.

'Actually, it might be better, Gwen, if you just took Ellie to—'

'That's fine,' Gwen interrupted hastily with a throwaway smile that didn't reach her eyes. 'I'll catch up with you both later.'

Roman waited until she had gone.

'She looked hurt then, when you told her to go,' Roman said slowly.

Rio's jaw clenched. *Tell me something I don't know.* '*She* is the mother of my child.'

Roman wondered if his twin was aware of

the pride in his voice or the challenge in his eyes. 'I did kind of work that one out,' he responded drily. 'So Mum was here, to meet her?'

Rio dragged a hand through his hair. 'Actually, she arrived looking for you. She is booked in for more surgery next Friday and she wanted to let you know,' he told his brother tersely.

'Is it—?'

'She said it's not serious but you know her.'

'So seeing Gwen and the baby must have made her happy... I am assuming that you two are together?'

'We will be.' Until he heard himself say it he hadn't really known that was what he wanted. But half-measure arrangements were no longer an option after last night. The recognition of that decision gave him a liberating lift and a moment's respite from the sense of impending doom that had descended when he saw his twin, the knowledge that there were no excuses left, he had to tell his brother the truth.

He'd known for days now that he had to do so, although Roman's sudden appearance had precipitated it.

'So what brings you here?'

*You're only delaying the painful moment,* Rio silently mocked himself.

'Thought I'd help out with the party, but I see you have it all in hand. So, does the surgery mean that Mum won't be here to host her party?' Roman looked at his obviously bewildered brother. 'It's July... You've forgotten about it, haven't you?'

Rio swore, which his twin took as a yes.

'I'll cancel it,' Rio said firmly.

'You can't do that—it's tradition and her way of saying thank you, even when she's not here in person.'

Rio muttered something indistinct about tradition that was probably unprintable, but Roman knew, they both did, that Rio would rise to the occasion. He could always be relied on to fulfil his duty and, on more than one occasion, Roman's too.

'So is the boyfriend going to be there to hold her hand again?' Roman asked.

'He's a nice guy, Roman,' Rio said as his twin sat down at the piano, lifted the lid and began a complex series of exercises. His brother had always struggled more than he had with their mother's ongoing relationship with a theatre director.

'This always did have a good tone.' Roman's hands fell away from the keys. 'And I'm still reserving judgement.'

'He's been around for two years now and she's very happy with him.'

'She'd better stay that way,' Roman growled and then changed the subject. 'So what's the story with you and Gwen?'

Rio exhaled. There was a story he had to tell his brother but it wasn't the one he was asking to hear.

'Just let me get this out before you…' Rio closed his eyes and clenched his jaw. 'Just let me get this out, Roman, before you say anything else.'

Gwen fed Ellie her breakfast before she popped her in the bath. Ellie loved bath time and Gwen, who like most single parents had become really expert at multitasking, had a micro shower with the door open so that she could still keep an eye on Ellie.

She had pulled on a pair of shorts and a cotton vest by the time Ellie was ready to leave the bath. A few minutes later they were both outside, Ellie wearing a cute play suit with a matching little sunhat and liberally plastered in sunscreen, though her skin had already developed a warm glow.

Gwen avoided the pool because she knew that Ellie would want to jump right in and instead made her way towards the dovecote that she had noticed when they arrived, armed with a bag of seeds she had seen stacked in the utility.

She sat on a bench and watched as Ellie threw seeds for the flock of white birds, thinking about how Rio had asked her to leave the room.

She knew that she was getting this out of all proportion—she had no right to feel hurt and excluded from a conversation between him and his brother.

But she did, and her throat thickened as she felt the push of tears behind her eyelids. If Rio hadn't so unexpectedly seemed to want her to stay before then sending her away, it might not have been so bad.

'Yes, bad bird, darling, very bad bird!' she yelled back in response to Ellie's finger-waving at one of the doves who the little girl had decided was *'very, very geedy'*.

'Well, what did you expect, Gwen?' she asked herself crossly before pausing to blow her nose on the tissue she fished out of her pocket. 'To be included in a private family meeting when you're not family?'

She knew she was an outsider here but the reminder had hurt more than she wanted to admit even to herself.

'All gone.' Ellie tipped her empty paper seed bag upside down.

Gwen smiled. 'Come on, that's enough sun for one morning, I think. How about some juice?'

Clapping happily, the toddler skipped ahead. They had come within sight of the driveway when a car sped around the bend in the drive with a squeal, kicking up gravel. Gwen grabbed Ellie and pulled her back into her body, reacting to instinct rather than any actual danger as she watched the speeding car vanish with one hand shading her eyes.

Rio's brother drove like a lunatic—or perhaps a very angry man?

'It's none of my business,' she said, addressing her remark to a cloud of dust, which was all that was left of the powerful car driven by Rio's twin.

Like every other room in the house, the kitchen of the beach house was built on a palatial scale. There were free-standing units in a bleached wood down one long wall, with an old-fashioned range that was gleaming and unused, presumably preserved from the original building, on the opposite wall. Gwen opened a cupboard in the massive island and pulled out a plastic tumbler, and watched as Ellie headed like a heat-seeking missile to the corner where a brand-new playhouse, complete with a garden filled with plastic flowers, took centre stage. Ellie marched straight to the little gate and stepped inside.

Gwen went across to the nearest of the massive fridges, and swung a door open. 'Orange, apple or *yummy* water, darling?' she asked, but Ellie was already engrossed in her make-believe game and didn't respond. Before she could repeat her question a figure appeared in the doorway to the adjoining utility room.

A choking sound escaped her throat and her

stomach took a sickening dive as she took in Rio's condition.

'Sorry, I'll just...' With a bloodied hand holding up an equally gory towel pressed to his face, Rio glanced towards Ellie, who continued to offer drinks from an invisible glass to dolls she had lined up in front of her.

'You carry on with Ellie. I was just washing up, then I might just...' He trailed off.

Rio's glance drifted back towards Ellie, who was animatedly talking to a teddy bear now.

'I don't want to alarm her.'

'You won't, although she might want to stick a plaster on you once she notices the blood.' Pity he wasn't so concerned about alarming me, Gwen thought acidly, trying to assess the damage behind the towel he was holding as she struggled to maintain at least the illusion of calm. 'What happened? Shall I call an ambulance?'

'*Dios*, no, it's just a nose-bleed. I'll wash up and get rid of this towel.'

Not fooled for an instant, she followed him into the utility area and asked her question in a firm tone that made it absolutely clear she expected an answer.

'What happened, Rio? And do not give me the nose-bleed story again. I'm not stupid!' Except she already was for imagining for one more moment that she could carry on pretending, even to herself, that she was not in love with Rio. The pretence had already grown thin, but seeing him standing there hurt and bleeding had peeled away the last of it, exposing the nerve of the truth. She had fallen for the father of her child, a man who would never love her back because he was too damaged from his own childhood experiences. 'What happened? Who did this?' There was only really one candidate to choose from but she wanted him to tell her. It was important to her for him to share at least this much.

'It's fine, don't fuss,' he said, his voice muffled by the towel.

'If you think all the machismo stiff-upper-lip stuff is going to impress me, you're very mistaken.' But then he wasn't trying to impress her, was he? She wanted to impress him; she wanted him to need her the way she needed him, and he wasn't going to, not ever.

'Let me see—'

'No!'

She ignored his protest and reached up to pull the towel away from his face. She swallowed a gasp, and thought, *Right, so your objectivity has gone out of the window; just wing it, girl!*

'That looks painful.' Turning so he couldn't see her own face, she walked across to one of the deep stone sinks inset into a smooth work surface made of the same material. 'I hope the other guy looks worse.' If it was Roman, as she fully suspected, he definitely would after she got her hands on him!

When Rio said nothing it only confirmed her suspicions. It seemed ironic that she had always wanted a sibling, but now she felt lucky she was an only child.

'Where's the first-aid kit?' It didn't even cross her mind that there wouldn't be one on his tick list when he had made this house a child-friendly haven.

'First door on the right.' He nodded to the open cupboard at the far end of the room. 'It doesn't matter. I'm fine,' he said, sounding irritated now.

She didn't have to feign anger to hide her feelings. 'You're an idiot!' she snarled, before muttering under her breath as she yanked the cupboard open. The label on the first-aid kit was in four languages just in case you made a mistake, and as she pulled it out and placed it on the work surface she opened her eyes wide.

'An EpiPen, *really*?' As a teacher, she knew a lot more than the general public about such things. 'You really did anticipate every disaster, didn't you?'

'Not me… I—'

'Yes, I know, you delegated the task,' she said in a flat voice. He might not give himself credit for getting this house ready for them, but she did. He hadn't personally painted the nursery or made every corner of this place as child friendly as was humanly possible, but he had instigated it all.

The effort he had made to accommodate a child into his life at incredibly short notice touched her deeply.

'What can I say? I was a Boy Scout,' he said, and she couldn't help but be aware of his intent stare following her as she selected the items she was looking for.

'Liar!' she denounced confidently. 'They'd have turfed you out after your first bad joke.'

Gwen gathered up the items she needed and walked back. Nothing in this place seemed to involve short distances. She sensed his eyes on her again and felt self-conscious. 'Sit down.'

Rather to her surprise, he did as he was told, straddling one of the tall stools that surrounded the peninsula work surface.

'This will probably hurt...' She took a deep breath and moved in closer, not realising until his thighs tightened on either side of her hips that she was standing between his legs. For once he didn't have the advantage of height, they were literally nose to nose, and the closeness was making her insides shudder. 'You more than me,' she added, avoiding looking him in the eyes, not liking the idea of what he might see there. She had her pride left if nothing else. 'Now, let me see...' It had never been more of a struggle to channel her inner unflappable schoolteacher than in this moment.

He lowered his hand and the towel, setting it to one side on the counter top, revealing the full extent of the damage, which she was hoping might not be as bad as it looked.

His jaw was red, his lip was split and starting to swell, his nose bloody and there was already the suggestion of a purplish bruise under one eye.

On one level she registered that it could be a lot worse, on another she was trying to function despite the strength of her emotional reaction to his pain, which was making it hard to get words past the contraction in her throat.

But presumably losing all sense of proportion was part and parcel of loving someone.

She glanced away, too afraid he might see the tears she could feel standing out in her eyes. 'Where else are you hurt?' she asked, her husky tone falling way short of the clinical one she was aiming for, but at least she wasn't openly crying.

'I'm fine.'

'Of course you are and it shows,' she came back sarcastically.

'Are you crying?' he asked in a strange voice—or then again it might have just been his lip.

'I am not crying.' She sniffed angrily. 'I am *angry*. You want to know why I'm angry?' Apparently he didn't; he was just watching her with a veiled expression in his dark eyes. Taken unawares, he didn't resist when without warning she took both his hands in hers and closely examined them. There wasn't a mark on them; no signs at all that he had defended himself.

She could think of only one person that Rio would not defend himself from.

Her eyes lifted, the blue light in them grim and hard, and Rio could see exactly what she was thinking—that his brother was a bastard. He knew he should really put her straight and explain that he was the one with the bastard credentials, but he found himself dreading seeing the sort of angry condemnation and contempt shining in her spectacular eyes right now directed at him. Even though he fully deserved it.

He acknowledged his uncharacteristic desire to please her with a faint frown, but his head hurt too much to delve any deeper into the reasons that it was so important to him for her to think he was one of the good guys.

Maybe the headache was a good thing, Rio mused grimly. He had enough complications in his life without looking for more...or maybe even inventing some. The priority he needed to focus on right now was being a good father, or at least not a bad one, and maybe persuading his twin to speak to him again. After all, Roman had only hit him the once, on his jaw, and, although he had a hell of a punch, the rest of the damage to Rio's face had happened when he'd hit the corner of the coffee table on his way down. It gave him a thin sliver of hope that he still might be able to salvage some sort of future relationship with his brother.

A sound of frustration escaped Gwen's clenched lips. 'So who did this? And do not say you walked into a door because, so help me, I will hit you myself! Oh, sorry,' she exclaimed with a wince of sympathy as she touched the alcohol swab to his cheekbone and he flinched.

Their eyes connected and her fingers found their way to the uninjured side of his face, curving tenderly around his cheek. 'Did your brother do this to you?'

'I deserved it!' The words almost seemed pushed out against his will and hung there in the air between them as a stunned and confused Gwen finished cleaning up his face.

Once she'd finished, she shoved the gauze and antiseptic back on the work surface. The twisting motion unsteadied her centre of gravity and his thighs immediately tightened around her and his big hands went to her waist.

Suddenly breathing was difficult, and thinking was even harder through the fog of sexual desire that seemed to fill the bubble of air around them, and all her liberated hormones were running riot.

She lacked the strength and willpower to avoid his steady hot stare, the raw glow in his eyes making her insides dissolve into a pool of liquid.

'Thank you.' Her voice sounded as if it belonged to someone else.

'No, thank you,' he came back smoothly.

The effort to stay still in his grasp brought beads of sweat to her upper lip, but she managed to break the grip of his stare to glance down momentarily at his hands that rested on her hips.

'What did you mean you *deserved* it?'

In her eyes violence was not an answer to anything. 'Also keep in mind that the martyr look on you is very unattractive.'

His hands dropped away, and he suddenly looked so bleak that she was seized by a powerful urge to take his face between her hands and kiss him, except theirs was not a relationship based on loving kisses, was it?

'Did your brother do this?' she asked again in a low, dangerous growl.

'Yes, but like I said I deserved it.' The muscular support of his confining thighs loosened and she stepped back, feeling quite ludicrously bereft.

The air hissed through her clenched teeth as she planted her hands on her hips and looked across at him. 'Did you even try and defend yourself?'

He flashed a grin and immediately winced, lifting a hand to his split lip. 'Have you never heard of turning the other cheek?'

'I'm surprised you have.'

Not resisting Roman's fury had not been a plan, just a reaction to Rio's belief that he deserved everything he got, but in the end it was what had stopped the escalation of the fight. If he had fought back Rio was sure his twin would have kept going to the death and Rio, with his newly acquired knowledge of what being a father meant to him, understood totally.

He watched Gwen stalk over to the fridge, pull out a tray of ice cubes and dump them into a clean towel. He loved the way she moved; there was an inherent grace to it that was all the more seductive for being totally unfeigned.

'It might help the bruising,' she said, thrusting the home-made ice pack at him. 'And maybe an aspirin.'

'I'd prefer a brandy.' He looked at her mouth, thinking that, actually, a kiss might work even better!

'It's not even midday.'

Her outrage struck him as hilarious under the circumstances, but laughing hurt. 'Fine, then a cup of tea would be nice. Shall we?' He nodded towards the doorway.

She walked ahead of him back into the kitchen where Ellie was no longer playing. Instead, she was curled up fast asleep in the garden of her playhouse, her thumb in her mouth.

Rio watched with tender eyes as Gwen scooped her up. At least his daughter had a clear conscience. He rubbed a hand down his jaw on the uninjured side of his face.

'I'll put her down in the nursery,' Gwen said.

# CHAPTER TEN

RIO NODDED AND watched her go, feeling the now familiar emotion tightening in his chest as he did so. The lightening of the heavy weight behind his breastbone had been only temporary. Once she had left the room it was back again.

He moved restlessly round the room. She was going to come back in a minute and then she'd be asking him questions again, and he'd end up telling her everything.

He felt he had to. The conviction that he shouldn't keep this from her any longer was deep but inexplicable. After all, it wasn't as though they were a couple, was it? They were just... His hands clenched as his handsome bruised features locked tight in a grimace of self-loathing and contempt.

*Dios mio*, they were not 'just' anything. That was the whole point, and if he'd needed evidence of it there was last night. He had gone past calling it mutual need, a chemical reaction. It was definitely *more* than that, but he didn't want more.

He wanted simple and clean cut.

Shaking his head and immediately regretting it, he headed for the living room. Tea might be nice in theory but he definitely needed something stronger and maybe two aspirin as well.

Ellie didn't wake as Gwen put her into her bed fully dressed; she was going to be hungry when she woke. Gwen kissed the air above her daughter's soft flushed cheek and pressed a button and the blackout blinds slid into place. Then she felt around to find the switch to turn on the night lights.

Her route back from the bedroom wing of the house to the kitchen took her past the open-plan living room that took up half the square footage of the entire building. She was determined to find out the truth about his fight with his brother if she had to physically drag it out of him.

She wouldn't accept a lie just because it made his life easier.

She had her argument in place if he was

difficult, which was virtually inevitable, she reflected grimly. If he argued that it wasn't any of her business he might be right—it wasn't. But Ellie was, and she had a right to know about anything that could impact on her daughter. She intended to tell him that she wouldn't allow their daughter to stay in an environment where violence was likely to flare up.

There had never been any violence in her home. Her father had many faults but that had not been one of them. Instead, her childhood had been the story of a relationship based on lies, and lies destroyed trust and self-respect, which was equally destructive.

She immediately felt guilty for likening Rio to her father even in a small way. Her father had always been a weak man and Rio was strong, but she knew environment mattered and it wasn't about toys or beautiful clothes, it was about feeling safe. Children soon learnt to recognise the lies and half-truths inside a house.

She and Rio might not be in a relationship as such—although quite frankly she didn't know *what* they were doing—but any decisions she made going forward had to be based on truth, not lies, and if he refused to talk to her then it was a deal-breaker for her.

She was determinedly stomping along the wide hallway back to the kitchen when a distinctive discordant sound of crashing piano keys from the living room brought her to an abrupt halt.

She retraced her steps to the set of open double doors, her first thought that Rio's twin had returned. *In which case, you're going to do what, Gwen? Tackle him single-handed because his stupid brother wouldn't defend himself?*

Her shoulders sagged in relief when she saw that Rio was alone.

'What are you doing?' she snapped as her agitated heart rate began to slow.

Rio was sitting at the grand piano, glass of brandy in one hand, the fingers of his other now running up and down some intricate scales. He looked up as she spoke.

'I couldn't find the tea.' He raised his glass.

She walked inside. 'I didn't know you played.'

He crashed the keys again, producing a discordant racket that made her wince before closing the lid and surging to his feet. Even in a space this size he was a dominant presence, projecting restless energy under the frustration.

'Roman is the musical one. I was never more than adequate, according to our music teacher. I was the one who was better at boxing, a nice irony, huh?' he said, touching his jaw. 'Roman was always too emotional—it must have been a lucky punch.'

'Or maybe you just stood there waiting for it and then took it like an idiot.' The image in her head made her as mad as hell. What on earth had he done that was so bad he felt he needed to be punished this way?

He gave her a sideways glance and didn't reply. 'Is Ellie okay?' he asked.

'She's fine, fast asleep. She missed her mid-morning nap, her routine is shot, so she'll sleep for a while.' Rio looked as if he needed to sleep too. She shook her head, impatient with herself. She had no idea why a tough man who was so obviously capable of looking after himself—except when it came to his twin—

brought out such crazy protective instincts in her. She wasn't in love, she was insane!

'So you want to know what is going on?' His shoulders lifted in one of his inimitable shrugs and he conceded, 'You have a right to, I suppose.'

Gwen had been prepared to tell him just that and now felt as if the wind had been taken out of her sails. 'I didn't think I had any rights,' she said, struggling to keep the resentment out of her voice and failing.

'Well, you're part of this family now, so you might as well know the worst about us.'

*Do not read too much into that,* she counselled herself firmly. *He just means you're family now because of Ellie.*

'This isn't our normal way of interacting, Roman and me... There is no history of this sort of thing.'

'By this sort of thing you mean him beating several shades of hell out of you.'

'I love it when you call a spade a bloody shovel, Miss Meredith.' He expelled a deep sigh through his nostrils and looked at her. 'Yes, that is what I mean.'

'And is it likely to happen again?'

'If Roman is to be believed I'm not likely to ever see him again—his last words to me were, "I'm finished with you!"' He gave a dry, unamused laugh. 'It sounded pretty convincing.' He continued to look at her, but as the moments stretched out Gwen had the impression he was not seeing her at all.

'That DNA match you saw nearly three years ago.'

His sudden words made her flinch. The memory of that day was etched deep in her psyche, and the wound was still barely scabbed over, even after all this time. 'Do we have to talk about that?' She was ashamed of her cowardly response but she couldn't help it.

'It's part of what happened today,' he said heavily.

'The argument was about your son?' she said gently. She could see the internal struggle on his face. This seemed to be something he had to tell her, or maybe he just had to confide in someone and she was here. But even if it was just an illusion it felt in that moment as if they were close.

'I don't have a son.'

A dozen meanings flashed through her head

and she blurted a response to the only one that really fitted his words and the terrible bleakness in his eyes.

'I'm so sorry.'

He stared at her, bewilderment etched into his face as she surged to her feet and rushed over to him, taking his big hands in her own.

'I can't imagine what it feels like to lose a child.' Her voice was husky with empathy and emotion as she thought with a shudder that she never wanted to know!

Without a word he flicked his hands over so that hers were now pressed between his. 'No one is dead, and I never had a son. Roman did—he does—but he didn't know.' He released her hands and touched his face, a rueful gleam in his eyes. 'Until I told him earlier.'

'You don't have a son?' Her mouth fell open, her knees sagged and she sat down on the leather recliner behind her. She could still hear the echo of his words vibrating in her head but they made no sense.

How could what he was saying be true?

'I don't understand.'

'Two weeks before we met in that bar I had a visit from…well, her name isn't important.

She'd had an affair with my brother two years before and apparently he'd proposed to her, which I have to admit fairly blew my mind at the time. I'd always thought Roman had the same mindset as—'

'You?'

'Well, anyway, she told me she was still married at the time but he didn't know.'

'She didn't tell him she was still married?'

Rio's hand, which had been raised to emphasise a point he'd been making, clenched and fell back to his side. 'Not until after his proposal. She had her reasons for that and they seemed right to her. Just as mine seemed right to me at the time. But that part is not my story to tell. Roman's proposal came with a demand that she get divorced immediately. She refused and...well, let's say their parting was not what you'd call amicable. A few weeks later, she discovered she was pregnant.'

'She passed the baby off as her husband's child?'

'He never knew about it because he died before she even knew she was pregnant. So fast forward now to the two weeks before you and I met in that bar. She turned up, made me promise not to tell Roman, then told me the whole story and explained that her son was seriously sick. He needed a bone-marrow transplant and his blood group was rare.'

Her eyes widened. 'The DNA results.'

He nodded. 'The thing about being an identical twin is that our DNA is identical, so I could donate instead of Roman.'

'You did?' He nodded. 'And the little boy… your nephew…he's okay now?'

'Fine, the last I heard.'

She gave a little sigh of relief.

'Marisa sends me a Christmas card and photos of the boy every year.'

He seemed unaware he had revealed the woman's name so Gwen didn't draw attention to it. He didn't need anything more to beat himself up over.

'Were you ever tempted to tell Roman? No, sorry.' She moved her head in a negative gesture. 'I shouldn't have asked.'

'Why not?' He seemed genuinely puzzled by her statement, which made her think how much their relationship had moved on during the past few days. 'And, yes, I was,' he admitted. 'There were several occasions where I was on the brink of breaking my word. If my brother hadn't taken himself off somewhere and turned into a hermit writer I might have done it, but instead it became an out-of-sight-out-of-mind situation.'

'But I don't understand—why didn't she just ask your brother to donate? Why didn't she tell him about his son?' She stopped, the irony of the recrimination in her voice hitting home. She was judging someone else…but what had this woman done that she hadn't?

She stared down at her clasped hands.

'I suppose pride played a part.' She looked up, a question in her cobalt-blue eyes. 'At the time she came to me, my brother was in a relationship, a pretty well-publicised one.'

'Oh…' Gwen felt a wave of sisterly sympathy for the other woman. 'It must have been hard for her bringing up a child alone, especially a poorly one.'

Rio watched the expressions drift across her soft features and felt a strong wave of protectiveness rise up in him.

'You managed.'

'That really isn't the same thing at all.'

'No, it isn't, because you had no support

network.' The idea of her parents abandoning her still made him see red and now he had a daughter of his own it seemed utterly inexplicable that Gwen had been cut off by the people who should have loved her the most. He knew that it didn't matter what Ellie did, he would always be there for her. 'And not much money to cushion you. Don't compare the situations, Gwen. You had to fend for yourself while she didn't have to worry about paying the rent.'

His unexpected defence brought a glow of pleasure to her face. 'But Ellie is not ill,' she pointed out, 'and I can't imagine how bad it would be if her life was in danger, especially when you have to make all the decisions yourself. That's the worst part really,' she mused.

'What is?' he asked, watching her closely.

'It's not just about the money though, gosh, yes, that helps. It's about not having someone to share the decisions with…someone to bounce ideas off and share the responsibilities with. Was she still in love with Roman, do you think?'

Rio shook his head. 'I'm not the expert on that subject,' he said. It was hard to be an expert on something when you'd spent your entire adult life running away from it. The love he'd seen up close and personal as a child had been a destructive force and the idea of embracing it had made as much sense to him as walking towards a tidal wave…knowing you would be completely helpless once you were in its grip.

Gwen's little glow of pleasure faded. Was she back to reality already? she wondered. The reality was that whatever future they had in front of them depended on her accepting the message in his words, and not expecting an iota more. Rio would never love her but he did love their daughter…which was what was most important, she reminded herself, ignoring the sinking feeling in her stomach.

'Is your brother still in a relationship?'

'Who knows?' he said with a shrug. 'He's walked out of the spotlight, and he's back to being his publicity-phobic self.'

'So he doesn't smile for the cameras like you, then?' she said, thinking sourly of all the online photos she'd seen of Rio with beautiful model types draped over him.

Rio didn't react to the jibe. 'It sounds as if his and Marisa's parting was particularly bitter and acrimonious. People say things in the heat of the moment that are hard to take back or forgive.'

Was he trying to say that he was sorry for the things he had said to her?

'You don't think your brother will forgive you, do you?'

A look of pain and self-recrimination moved across his face. 'No, I don't.'

'Maybe the question you *should* be asking yourself is would you forgive him if the roles were reversed?'

She caught an arrested look on his face before he turned and walked through the open doors onto the patio. She watched him standing there dragging his hand through his already tousled hair for a moment before joining him.

The smell of lavender and lemon thyme was strong in the warm air.

'He's my twin. I'm not suggesting we have some magical connection but in the past we have always been each other's support network, no matter the distance between us. I resented him walking away and leaving me with the business, and we should have had a bust-up about that then rather than let it fester. Who knows? It might have cleared the air between us… But then I was already feeling guilty…'

'So that's a yes. You would forgive him if the roles were reversed.'

He looked at her then with an almost smile. 'But I'd have hit him harder first.'

'So if you'd forgive him why wouldn't he forgive you—in time?'

He barked out a harsh laugh. 'You like happy-ever-after endings.'

She pushed away the knowledge that she was not likely to have her happy ever after because you couldn't force someone to love you. 'Doesn't everyone?' she said lightly. From this side of him his profile was unblemished and, of course, perfect. You couldn't see the damage to his face, but her stomach muscles fluttered because she knew it was there.

'Is it still hurting?'

'I took the aspirin.'

Squinting, she looked up at him, lifting a hand to shade her eyes from a blazing sun that had climbed high in the sky. 'And the brandy.' There was a teasing note in her voice.

His eyes drifted over her fair skin, where she knew that a scattering of freckles had appeared across the bridge of her nose. His hand lifted briefly before it dropped back to his side, and she wondered if he'd had a sudden impulse to reach out and touch her skin.

'Come and sit in the shade.' Concern lent his tone roughness. 'The entire place is wired for sound so we'll hear Ellie if she wakes.'

'Oh, she'll sleep for a while yet,' Gwen said, following him across to an area that was shaded by a canopy. She hesitated to take the seat beside him on the sofa, but felt it would look too obvious if she sat half a mile away from him.

Nothing essentially had changed; she'd just faced up to a fact that she had been hiding from. He wasn't going to return her love.

'Your brother mentioned a party.'

'Ah, *the* party. My mother holds one here every year. A celebration of her divorce and a thank you to all the friends who stood by her through the years despite the best efforts of my father to alienate her from them. Yes, this is a family where we actually celebrate divorce.' He drained the last finger of brandy and looked at her over his glass, as if trying to judge her reaction.

'If my mum ever decided to divorce my father I'd celebrate.'

The admission made him laugh. 'So you don't believe in the marriage myth either.'

'I didn't say that.' She hesitated—did he want to hear this? What the hell? She wanted to say it, so she would. 'I know the statistics, but I don't see why it shouldn't be a goal... I don't know what makes a *perfect* marriage or even if such a thing exists, but I do know what is essential before a marriage can work.'

'And that would be?'

She responded without hesitation. 'There has to be ongoing open communication. You have to be able to talk to the person you spend the rest of your life with. I don't mean you can't be different—you shouldn't ever lose your individuality—but I suppose you should at least share common values. And there has to be honesty and trust.' She firmly believed that trust once lost was almost impossible to regain.

'You have obviously put some thought into the subject. So love is optional for you?'

She shook her head vigorously, defiance edging her words as she insisted, 'Love is essential but I don't think you can ever be complacent about it. It needs careful nurturing, and it won't survive if you lose all the other things along the way.'

As the silence stretched she began to feel embarrassed for sounding off like that, for giving such an intense response to a casual question. He was probably wondering how to change the subject.

'When Roman and I were kids we both vowed that we'd never get married or have kids of our own. I think the kid part scared Roman more than me because he was always afraid that he had more of our father in him and he always said why take the risk passing on tainted genes?'

A little sound of horror that escaped her lips brought his eyes to her face. He sketched a quick smile that left his dark eyes sombre as their gazes met and despite the matter-of-fact delivery she could feel the pain behind his words, the memories that had influenced his young life and still did.

'So I never thought that Roman would really want to know...'

'You thought you were protecting him,' she breathed softly.

He shook his head. 'Did I? I really don't know but back then I had no idea, not the faintest concept of what having a child feels like. But now I do and I've deprived him of the opportunity of having the same joy.'

The simple sincerity in his words made her eyes fill with tears.

'Roman always said marriage was a prison and I agreed with him. I should have realised when Marisa said he'd proposed to her that he'd already moved on, had managed to escape the past even if I hadn't.' The self-contempt in his voice was corrosive.

'But my mother's marriage *was* a prison.'

She covered his hand that lay on the table with her own. 'I think your mother is a very strong person to come through it as happy as she obviously is.'

Rio looked from the small hand on his to her face, and the muscles along his jawline quivered. 'She is, but she still won't go back to the house, our estate, even though he's dead.'

Sympathy softened Gwen's blue eyes. Jo had given herself and her sons a new life but it had taken courage. She found herself wondering what her life would have been like if her mother had refused to tolerate her father's infidelities and left him years ago.

Perhaps none of us ever escaped our past, she mused. Certainly these revelations about his childhood explained so much about Rio, especially his avoidance of committed relationships. A deep sadness rose up in her for him and his brother, and an anger and disgust for the parent who had scarred them this way.

'How old were you?'

'When they split, twelve, when he died we were twenty. The years in between, or at least until we were eighteen, we had to spend alternate holidays with him. He used to try and get information out of us about Mum, who was she seeing, that sort of thing, and the things he said about her…'

Gwen just nodded and didn't tell him she already knew about that from Jo. She was touched by the fact he was confiding in her and trying desperately hard not to read too much into it.

'He wasn't just toxically jealous—he was coercive and controlling.' The look of revulsion that crossed his face made her heart twist in her chest with a painful pulse of empathy.

It seemed to her that although their mother had escaped from him, the twins hadn't. What a terrible thing to use your own children as weapons, though sadly she knew that it was not as rare as it should be.

'It was a relief.'

She realised he was looking at her as though he expected her condemnation.

'It was a relief when he died,' he expanded.

'Of course it was.' It seemed to her that guilt was Rio's factory setting. 'So when he died you were finally free?'

He hesitated, the direct question resurrecting his hauteur that Gwen recognised now as a defence mechanism to keep people at arm's length.

Their eyes met and the ice in Rio's gaze warmed and vanished. There was something about her quiet interest, the total lack of prurience, that made him continue.

'Free of him but not entirely. Over the years he had used our inheritance as a stick to beat us with, threatening to cut us off so often that we both assumed that he had. We both made our own plans. Roman was in his second year at Oxford, I'd taken the year out and was working on an outback station in the Northern Territory.'

Gwen blinked. 'I can just see you on horseback.'

He smiled, but it faded almost instantly. 'Then we found out he'd left us it all anyway, the family estate and the money and also the private equity firm that he had founded. He was a bastard, but a bastard who knew how to make money. So in a way he found a way to control us after all—we had to learn fast.' He stopped mid-sentence, an arrested, self-conscious expression freezing his features into a shocked frown.

Where had his initial reluctance to explain the skewed dynamic of his definitional family background to her gone? He'd had to fight, to begin with, against the habit of a lifetime to reveal the facts he felt circumstances decreed she should know.

Now here he was, acting as though he were in a therapy session giving her an unrequested tour of his murky childhood and psychological flaws. 'Sorry, this is not really relevant—you must be a sympathetic listener.' She was certainly a non-judgemental one, which was a lot more than he deserved.

'So you worked together, you and Roman?'

'Initially I thought we made a good team. Until he left.'

And now he was a man shouldering all the responsibility, Gwen thought. 'You miss him.'

His eyes slid from hers and she could almost see him retreating from her as he sketched a quick smile. 'We have never lived in one another's pockets or finished each other's sentences.'

'So what made your mother leave your father in the end?'

'Actually this house was the final straw. It had belonged to her family and she'd inherited it. In the early days we came here on holidays regularly, but then my father took against it simply, I think, because she loved it, and then he arranged the sale of it behind her back and he told her to sign on the dotted line.'

Gwen watched as a thoughtful expression

drifted across his face as though he was re-living a moment in the past.

'She said it was like waking up after a long nightmare. She ripped up the contract, grabbed us and, the way she tells it, a bag of knickers, phoned the best divorce lawyer she could and brought us here. The rest is history. Oh, and the lawyer will be one of the guests at the party. They are a pretty eclectic bunch but I think you'll like them.'

'I assumed that you were going to cancel…' She stopped. 'I'll still be here, will I?'

'It seems the ideal opportunity to introduce you to the people who matter to me, and Ellie, of course.'

'You're going to go public about us?'

The brow on the uninjured side of his face lifted. 'I considered sliding down my seat in the car and hiding from it all but…'

The teasing reminder of what she'd done at school to avoid those parents made her flush.

'Perhaps,' Rio said, watching her closely, seeing the wariness in her eyes, 'I should be asking you if you're all right with going pub-lic.'

'Would it matter if I said no?'

'Yes, of course it would.'

His response looked as if it surprised her.

'I'm not ashamed I'm a father. I'm proud of Ellie and of you for making such a good job of it.' Her flush of pleasure at this unexpected praise hadn't subsided when he added, 'But you're not alone any more. I'm not asking you to marry me.'

The colour seeped from her cheeks, leaving just two circles of pink on each cheekbone as her lashes came down. 'I didn't think you were.'

'I really doubt if I could fulfil your criteria for one half of a good marriage.' He'd be very surprised if any man could, but he found he really didn't want any man other than him trying. 'But I want to be part of your and Ellie's lives.'

Gwen knew he really meant just Ellie. She was only included because they came as a package deal. She ignored the heavy weight that had taken up residence behind her breastbone and said nothing; the aching lump in her throat would have made it hard anyway.

'I think we should live together for Ellie's sake.'

Gwen's expression hardened. She half rose but he caught her hand and after a moment she subsided. 'Live a lie, you mean,' she said numbly. Everything in her was repelled by the idea of taking the first step on the road her own mother had chosen.

'No lies, just an open and honest relationship. We both have Ellie's best interests at heart and I don't want to be an every-other-weekend dad.'

'By open, do you mean—?' She found she couldn't even finish the sentence.

'As it is I really don't want to sleep with another woman, but I don't want to make any unrealistic promises to you that I might not be able to keep. I respect you too much for that.'

His matter-of-fact confession of possible future infidelity sent a cold chill through her body, but Rio seemed oblivious to her reaction and continued to outline his plan in more detail.

'I own a house in London, and the one next door has just gone on the market. It has a lovely walled garden and there is a fantastic school close by. You could move in and we could see how things go, and who knows?

We might end up getting on so well we knock down the partition wall.'

'Or you might move your girlfriend in next door,' she said flatly, fighting the childish impulse to stamp her foot and yell, *I don't want your respect. I want your love, you stupid man!*

She had dreamt of receiving proposals but not this one!

'Or *my* boyfriend might not want you as *our* next-door neighbour,' she added sweetly, and she felt a surge of savage satisfaction when she saw his expression darken, while fire not ice filtered into his dark stare.

He suddenly looked very dangerous and she knew it wasn't an illusion but, instead of feeling like running for the hills or at least closing her mouth over further inflammatory comments, Gwen felt a rush of exhilaration.

'I think that it's back to the drawing board, Rio, because that idea absolutely does not fly with me. I'm happy for you to have access to Ellie but I am not living a lie for anyone.'

There was a look of shock on his face, as though he wasn't used to anyone saying no to him, which he probably wasn't, but Gwen didn't feel sorry for him because she was too busy feeling utterly furious with him.

As the worst effects of the flash of mind-freezing fury sparked by the image Gwen's words had planted in his head, of her in bed with some other man, subsided, Rio recovered his voice.

'I'm not asking you to live a lie.' She was twisting everything, making it sound as though he hadn't thought it through, but he had.

'Just live next door to you, I know, and be on tap for sex when there is nothing better on offer. They used to call that being a mistress.' Her chin went up and she glared at him through fiery cobalt eyes. 'Well, I am not mistress material and I have no idea where you got the idea I was.'

'Believe me, if I had a mistress it wouldn't be one who takes offence at absolutely nothing. At least I have a plan! What do you suggest we do?' he asked, feeling incredibly frustrated that she had turned down his idea point-blank, without even considering it.

'I don't have to *do* anything. Ellie is my daughter. I'm not going to give up my job, my life and move halfway around the country just so that it's more convenient for you.' Hands on the arms of the sofa, she pushed herself up.

'So are you holding out for marriage, then? Is that what this is all about?'

The sneer in his voice did it. She twirled back on him, for once able to look him in the face as she levelled her shaking finger at his broad chest. 'Obviously I'm desperately tempted,' she snapped with withering sarcasm.

Rio, who had regretted the words the moment they left his lips and blamed them on the image of her nameless future lover still residing in his head, felt the regret fade as she spoke. He reached up, his fingers curling around the wrist above the wagging finger.

She froze but didn't resist the light pressure he exerted to draw her downwards. Her only reaction was to reach out and brace a hand against the arm of the sofa to stop her body simply collapsing against him; as it was he was close enough to feel the heat off her body and inhale the scent of her skin.

One hand curved across the back of her head, fingers digging deep in her hair as he brought her face in close, feeling the tremor that ran through her body. Above the dull hammer thud of his heartbeat he could hear the soft hiss of her uneven breathing, and feel her warm breath on his face. Only a thin rim of bright blue remained visible around her massively dilated pupils.

This wasn't the normal scratching of a carnal itch; it was as if something in her connected with a deep inner emptiness inside him, and he wanted to fill it with her warmth. As he stared into her eyes the hunger inside him flared white-hot and any anger that had been in him seeped away as the tide of hot, humid desire rushed in to replace it. What shocked him the most was that in the middle of all the lust a tenderness surfaced. She looked so confused and so lost—the idea of being a person who would take advantage of that confusion repelled him.

With a growled imprecation of self-disgust he released her. It was so sudden and the sense of anticlimax so extreme that Gwen gasped like someone who had just fallen into ice water and staggered a couple of steps before she regained her balance.

She just stood there looking at him, her

plump lips swollen as if he had just kissed them, and temptingly parted as she dragged in air in gulping gasps like someone who was drowning.

The strength of the passions he stirred inside her with such insultingly effortless ease was terrifying and yet it was also exciting. She didn't know who she was; the swift shift from angry resentment to all-consuming passion was utterly disorientating. She ought to be grateful he had stopped, that he hadn't kissed her, but she wasn't. She was angry.

She was aching.

She buried her humiliation deep behind a blank mask. 'I'll go and check on Ellie.' She turned, head held high and narrow back straight, and walked back into the house.

The unstudied provocation of the gentle sway of her hips distracted Rio enough to make him forget to make allowances for his injuries as he dragged a frustrated hand down the bruised and battered side of his face.

He held in a groan of pain behind the barrier of his clenched white teeth.

# CHAPTER ELEVEN

FIFTY PUNISHING LAPS of the pool hadn't even taken the edge off his frustration, although Rio hoped that if he punished his body enough it would stop punishing him or maybe the voice in his head would just switch off. Even turning the volume down would be a help at this stage.

He swam to the side and put his hands on the tiled surround to heave himself out and changed his mind. Falling backwards into the water again, he allowed himself to sink to the bottom, staying there long enough to feel the burn in his lungs before he kicked for the surface and the sparkle of the rejected multi-coloured lights.

He broke the surface gasping, his chest heaving, and wondering if maybe the pool had been a mistake. The memories of the previous night were still too fresh in his mind.

*Well, they're going to stay that way, aren't they, Rio, while you carry on reliving every glorious minute of it?* He shook his head, sending a shower of silver droplets outwards onto the water, pebbling the still surface.

*Let it go,* counselled the voice in his head, but it wasn't easy advice to take when he didn't want to let anything go and desperately wanted a repeat performance.

He leaned back, letting the water support his body, and he stayed that way for several moments, arms outstretched in a crucifix position, staring through half-closed lids at the stars dotted in the midnight blanket of the night sky. Except it wasn't midnight, it was three a.m. and yet again he hadn't had a moment's sleep.

With a small grunt of effort he struck out, still on his back, his body silently cutting through the water. His arms and legs worked in unison as he cleaved straight as an arrow through the water, pushing himself to the limit and silently counting out each turn.

After another fifty lengths he stopped, treading water before he finally hauled himself out. He stood there on the rim of the pool, his lean brown body almost invisible in the darkness, water streaming down his face and body, looking at nothing through the blur of water droplets that pooled on the ends of his lashes. The vigorous exercise had not cleared his head or tamed his body.

He closed his eyes, head back; his chest lifted in a deep soundless sigh. If he couldn't get rid of it he had to live with it, he told himself as he headed for the outdoor shower. He revolved under the cold spray until all trace of pool water was long gone and his skin was icy from the prolonged exposure that he hoped would offer him some respite from the relentless, pounding desire that defied the iron control he had come to take for granted. Rio was tolerant of weakness in others but not in himself, and he hadn't allowed his body to rule him since his hormonal teens.

He shook the moisture off his hair before he used both hands to smooth off the excess, then grabbed his towel, looped it across his shoulders and headed back to the house.

They had spoken, just not to each other, barring the odd 'please' and 'thank you' or frigid 'excuse me', while Ellie had glowed with all the attention that came her way partly to compensate for the silences between her parents.

It was childish, and he knew it, but he still hadn't been prepared to back down first and say sorry or whatever it took to thaw the frosty atmosphere.

The only full sentence she had directed at him was when she had asked if he'd like to put Ellie to bed. Had this been her way of meeting him in the middle, an olive twig rather than a branch? It was only a possibility that had occurred to him after the fact and then it was too late. Gwen had taken herself off to bed soon afterwards.

He didn't bother turning on the lights as he padded through the open-plan living area. The tiled floor was warm underfoot with the heat retained from the day's sun, even though the ambient temperature had been lowered to a comfortable level by the air conditioning.

He headed towards the bedroom wing, where the doors of the empty suites were open. One door beside his own was closed, and he found his feet stopping outside it.

He stayed there, struggling with the battle going on inside him, a struggle that was etched into the strong lines of his lean, sculpted features. His emotions were written on his face but there was no one around to hide them from. Gwen was behind the door. He stared at it, wondering if she was asleep or if she had lain awake thinking of him. He could picture her curled up in bed, her glorious hair spread out over the pillow.

What would she say if he knocked?

A sigh slipped from his mouth. He valued his freedom; he liked being answerable to no one. Yes, he was a father now but that wasn't going to change, because it didn't need to.

The problem was every time he looked at Gwen, when he smelt her skin, or touched her, a fragment of the wall of his carefully compartmentalised life crumbled, and he needed to stay in control.

What the hell was he doing?

Impatient with his own thoughts, and teeth clenched in a fierce grimace, he turned to walk further down the corridor to his room when the sound of a door opening stopped him. He swung back, his heartbeat accelerating, and she was standing there, all shocked big eyes, soft mouth and glorious tumbling hair. The tee shirt she was wearing clung to the high contours of her rounded breasts and just about reached the tops of her thighs, revealing the lovely tanned length of her long legs.

Like his brother's punch, he didn't try and block the flame of desire that scorched through him. He doubted that it would have made a difference even if he had; it would have been like trying to turn the tide with the power of his mind.

Shock nailed Gwen to the spot. 'I... I... wanted...' Her voice drifted away, and she forgot what she wanted to say. 'Milk...?' she said faintly, trying to think past the will-sapping fog of desire in her brain.

She swallowed, her eyes dropping as her gaze slid down the lean length of his powerful body. She had no time to prepare any defences and couldn't hide what she was feeling.

'Oh, my God,' she whispered, the words dragged from the deepest part of her as the fight drained out of her. She might as well have fought her own DNA than tried to fight the way he made her feel.

For several heartbeats neither of them moved, then they fell into one another, kissing with a desperation that was almost feral in its intensity. Her hands were locked behind his neck as his hands moved over her shaking body, moulding her bottom and sliding down her slim thighs, then up under the hem of her nightshirt.

Gwen gasped, her head falling back as his lips made slow progress up the curve of her throat, and she arched into him.

Then her eyes filled with guilt and she lifted her head, pulling back a little as she laid her hand on his cheek. 'Your poor mouth.' She raised herself on tiptoe and kissed the corner of his injured mouth. 'I don't want to hurt you.'

He flashed a fierce smile and took her face between his hands. 'I'm a fast healer.' Holding her gaze, he very slowly fitted his mouth back to hers.

The slow, dreamy, sensuous kiss was blissful torture. His eyes burned with need as his head lifted, and the predatory glitter made her legs weak with lust.

'You're so beautiful,' he rasped with a strained grin before he trailed a kiss down her jaw. Then, reaching the corner of her mouth, he added, 'Are you going to invite me in?'

She didn't say a word, she just looked at him, silent longing glowing in her eyes. Rio was stunned by the need building inside him. The strength of it was like nothing he had ever known before.

She turned and Rio followed her into the bedroom and over to the bed, where the covers were thrown back and the pillows all over the place as though she had done a lot of tossing and turning. He found himself pleased that he hadn't been the only one suffering.

Her eyes were locked on his as she sat on the edge of the bed. He walked over to her and, still holding her eyes, caught the edge of the nightshirt. Without a word she lifted her arms and he pulled it over her head.

Gwen heard his raw gasp. Her eyes had drifted closed and she couldn't open them; they felt heavy, her entire body infused with languid weakness.

She felt the bed give a little as he joined her there, drawing her down beside him until they lay thigh to thigh, face to face beside one another.

The first skin-to-skin contact drew a deep shuddering sigh from her, and her eyes opened. She raised her head and kissed him on the mouth, telling herself that she didn't care about the future. All she cared about was now and being with this beautiful man who she loved.

He was stroking her everywhere, and she was just holding him. It felt as if she were floating outside herself but she had never felt so aware of her body, or so in tune with it.

'I want to taste you…all of you…' He slid down her body, his mouth warm and moist, his tongue drawing raw gasps of pleasure from her parted lips as she arched to his touch.

He drove her close to the edge twice before he responded to her pleas and allowed her to guide him into the tight warmth between her thighs.

'Look at me, Gwen. I want to see your face,' he urged. He was never a selfish lover, but she thought he'd never taken so much care with the pleasure he was giving her before.

They moved together, their gasps and moans becoming one part of the perfect whole until the frantic final moments of pushing to reach the heights. The release when it came shook her to her core…the waves of pleasure reaching her curling toes and continuing to rock her as she clung to him, pressing her face into his shoulder.

Finally he flopped over onto his back and lay there, his flat belly sucking in oxygen, his chest rising and falling until his breathing slowed, and he turned his head and looked at her.

'Shall I stay?'

She looked at him, her loving gaze moving over his beautiful bruised face, and she felt a debilitating kick of warm desire.

'Yes,' she murmured, rolling towards him, fitting herself to his hard angles. She hated the idea of him being in the next room, and being in the next house was even more unacceptable to her.

She was nervous in the run-up to the party, but not as much as she had expected. Then again, there hadn't been much time to get nervous, only forty-eight hours. Luckily Rio's mother had organised the catering, and all Gwen had had to do was open the door to the small local firm.

Though actually opening the door to anyone, and letting the world in, had not been an inconsequential thing. It had effectively shattered the feeling of isolation from the world that had enveloped Gwen ever since they'd arrived at the beach house.

Up to that point, for all the contact they'd had with the outside world they could have been on their own desert island, with the exception of the rather dramatic interruption afforded by first Jo's fleeting visit, and then Roman's.

Now the world was here, or at least a very small proportion of it. Rio had said it would be an eclectic mix of people and he hadn't been inaccurate. The majority Jo had met through her charity work, and there were some well-known faces among them. Gwen's own concerns about what to wear had been dispelled as soon as people started to arrive, dressed in a wide variety of styles. When Rio had said she could wear *anything* she liked she had accused him of being unhelpful, but it turned out he was actually being literal.

At the moment he was being invisible. She glanced around with a slight furrow between her feathery brows, realising that she hadn't seen him for half an hour or so. He'd stayed by her side as he'd promised during the introductions and then left her to sink or swim. She was mostly swimming, to be honest, and if anyone was curious when Rio introduced her as *'Gwen, Ellie's mum'*, they were polite enough to hide it.

Ellie was represented by a framed photo that everyone admired. It was the same photo that Rio had emailed his mother at her request.

Rio had told Gwen that Jo was ecstatic about being a grandmother and she couldn't wait to meet her granddaughter again.

Ellie herself was in bed and asleep. Rio had agreed readily enough when Gwen had said she wasn't having her daughter paraded for inspection as well as herself.

Gwen joined in the ripple of applause when their most instantly recognisable guest, who was sitting at the piano playing requests, played the opening chords of one of his hits. He'd aged pretty well for a member of an iconic eighties rock band that had not been known for its moderation.

He was being accompanied by a woman wearing a fashionable jumpsuit who had arrived with her saxophone. Apparently, her day job was in the head office of a charity, although she looked like a model.

There were at least three men and a woman wearing jeans and a few men in tailored trousers and shirts like Rio and a smattering of women in formal evening gowns. A few were dressed as Gwen was, somewhere in between the two. In the end she had chosen a mid-length silk shift in a dramatic violet shade, cut high at the neck and dipping into a deep V at the back. She had worn it for every 'special occasion' event for the past three years but nobody here would know that, and she was just glad she had thrown it into her case as an afterthought.

She responded to a comment about her shoes from a woman whose name she had forgotten, and agreed they looked good but they were killing her.

'Where's Rio got to?' the woman asked.

'Not sure.'

'The last time I saw him he was with Rach and she'd had a few too many glasses of fizz, so the poor man will need rescuing.'

Now there was a name she remembered and the last time she had seen him with Rach he hadn't looked much as if he needed rescuing. On the contrary, he'd looked as if he was enjoying himself as the *tactile* curvaceous blonde in the sequined minidress had laughed her head off at something he had just said.

Gwen made her way around the outside of the room. She had been checking on Ellie regularly all evening and it occurred to her that maybe Rio had too. His absence could simply be explained by the fact that she had woken.

A smile tinged with pride tugged at the corners of her lips. Despite all her misgivings Rio was really trying to be a good father— actually better than trying. He *was* a good father. Anyone seeing them together would know that. Being a single parent, knowing that, if anything happened to her, Ellie would be alone had been a nightmare that had regularly woken Gwen in the middle of the night in a cold sweat.

She hadn't had that nightmare since her first day here. Even if she knew that the only place Rio wanted her was in his bed, he genuinely wanted Ellie in his life. Gwen told herself she had everything but his love, and while Ellie was safe she could live with that.

When it was fifteen minutes past and he still hadn't reappeared her conviction that he was trying to settle their daughter increased, so Gwen decided to check out her theory and relieve him. She managed to slip away unnoticed and once in the tiled hallway she stepped out of the admired heeled sandals that were murdering her feet. Dangling them from her fingers, although she didn't think she'd actually get them back on again, she hurried along the corridor.

Rio's job would be a hell of a lot tougher if he hadn't surrounded himself with a team of people he could rely on, people he was happy to delegate responsibility to. This was especially important after his brother had left for pastures new.

Up to this point he had never absented himself from work for this length of time, but he'd known that if he wanted to prove to Gwen he was serious about being part of Ellie's life he had to show his willingness to adapt, show he didn't want to be an absentee father.

He had not gone totally off grid; he had left an emergency number, but had made it clear to his second in command that when he said emergency he meant emergency.

So when the private number had buzzed earlier, the timing had been lousy but he had known he had to answer it.

He was glad he had. The conference call had certainly had its tense moments but half an hour later he was able to sink back into the padded swivel chair, happy in the knowledge that a costly disaster had been averted.

The noise from the party was reduced to a gentle hum in the book-lined study where he had used to sit in a corner with a book, watching his mother write in one of the journals she kept. One day, she used to tell him, she'd turn the words on the paper into a book—he wondered idly if she still intended to.

Spinning around, he was about to lever himself out of the chair when a breathy voice made him freeze.

'Rio…so there you are, you naughty man. I've been looking for you everywhere.'

He sighed. Some people just shouldn't drink and Rachel was one of them. 'Hello, Rach, what brings you here?' The thing with Rachel was that, while perfectly charming when she was sober, when she was drunk the young widow was an octopus. He wasn't the only one of her friends to notice that she was drunk a lot of the time these days and as yet she hadn't admitted to herself that she had a problem.

'Were you waiting for me, darling?' she slurred as she swayed into the room on perilously high heels.

Rio's sympathy was currently tinged with impatience. He really didn't have time for this; he needed to get back to the party and Gwen.

'No, I wasn't.'

'Oh, I think you were… Are we going for that swim now?' She gave a little giggle. 'Oh, yes, that would be lovely. I don't have a swimsuit, but you don't mind that, do you, darling?'

'*Not* a good idea, Rach.' Alarmed by the speed with which this farce was developing and the potential for it becoming something worse, Rio moved forward, but was too late to stop her pulling down the zip on her sparkling minidress. The back sagged open and it slid half off her shoulders.

'*Dios mio*, Rachel, you need a coffee.'

She stood there swaying, her colour suddenly not good. He noticed the tears standing out in her eyes and his mood softened as he realised that on one level she had to know that she was making a fool of herself, and yet he and everyone else would carry on making allowances for her because you did cut some slack for someone who'd nursed the love of their life through a terrible terminal illness before being tragically widowed in their twenties.

'No, I need to lie down...' She blinked and the tears were gone and her seductive smile reappeared. 'Lie down with me, Rio...' She made a grab for his shirt and for a moment it seemed as if it was the only thing holding her up.

Grinding out a curse, he moved his hand to her waist to stop her slithering to the floor. She didn't, but the dress finally surrendered to gravity and lay like a pile of chain mail at her feet.

It was into this scene that Gwen walked, and his first reaction was relief that there was someone to help him cope with his sad, drunk friend.

He was about to say, *Thank God you're here,*

when he saw her face, white as chalk, and her blue eyes frosted with suspicion and accusation.

He was ready to concede that at first glance this could look like an incriminating scenario, but she had to *want* to read it that way, he decided grimly, to carry on believing that. Unless, of course, Gwen really thought he was the sort of person who was likely to take advantage of a drunk and vulnerable woman.

Reacting to the direct hit to his pride inflicted by Gwen's silent accusation, he found that, instead of appealing for help, he'd angled a look of challenge at her. He was almost daring her to say what she was thinking as the woman he was supporting snuggled up closer to him, the sense of betrayal he was feeling stoking his spiralling anger.

She said nothing, but her silence spoke volumes. Rio remembered his father's toxic silences, meant to punish, and they had. They could last weeks after he had thought he'd discovered his wife having a non-existent affair that had been proven in his distorted eyes by a glance or even on one occasion, Rio remembered, a pair of shoes!

If Gwen could not trust him, that was her problem. He would not validate her jealousy by offering excuses, or demean himself by doing so.

But as she walked away, still without having said a word, he saw that Gwen was carrying her shoes, the same shoes he had earlier imagined her wearing with nothing else on as he carried her to their bed.

He still had Rachel in his arms, and getting her onto the couch while evading her attempt to grab his crotch did not improve his temper. Luckily for him the next person to appear in the doorway did not look at him with accusing eyes; instead, she was sympathetic and grateful. Rachel's friend May had come looking for her.

Her face was solemn as she told Rio to return to the party; she would stay with Rachel, she said.

'This isn't the real her, you know,' she added as Rio turned to go.

'I know, but she needs help. She can't go on like this.'

The other woman sighed. 'I agree. Maybe it's time we all stopped covering for her, before it's too late.'

Minutes beforehand, Gwen had been able to circulate and feel as if she belonged with all these amusing, entertaining people. Now, as she returned from Rio's study, she felt awkward and out of place, and whatever had made her feel she belonged, it was pathetic.

*She* was pathetic for believing that Rio had changed, not that he loved her, she wasn't *that* deluded, but that he cared a little, that fatherhood had changed him from the man whose socks had a longer lifespan than his lovers and probably more respect from him too.

He had actually had the gall to look angry at *her*! As if he were the victim... Her jaw quivered as she bit down on her full lower lip. Six feet five inches of muscle made a very unlikely victim in her book!

A smile painted on her face, she drifted around the room feeling the anger and disillusion building inside her. It hadn't been what he'd been doing—well, actually it had, she admitted, experiencing a flash of nausea as she recalled the scene she had walked in on— but the thing that was the deal-breaker was the fact that he hadn't been willing to unbend enough to explain himself, offer her the reassurance she needed.

Would she have believed him if he'd given her an explanation? She pushed away the irrelevant question, because he hadn't given her the option and she hadn't been forced to face her real fear, which was that she'd turn into her mother, pathetic enough to believe any lie in order to stay with the man she loved.

The worst part, the part that scared her the most, was that she had so badly wanted Rio to tell her it wasn't what it looked like, the same way she had seen her own mother beg time after time, swallowing her husband's stories, where somehow he was always the victim.

The idea that she might turn into a woman that her daughter would one day be ashamed of filled her with a stomach-clenching horror.

She hid her misery behind a wide smile, but

no one seemed to notice that her laughter was brittle and her eyes too bright.

She was conscious of Rio returning, not that he made any attempt to talk to her. He probably expected *her* to apologise to him.

Of the blonde there was no sign—not until Gwen watched the last of the taxis drive away and she thought she saw a distinctive blonde head in the back of one.

Finally the last guest was dispatched and the last crate of crockery loaded up by the ultra-efficient caterers. Gwen wandered back to the kitchen, which showed no sign of their temporary occupation, and stood watching through the window as the tall figure walking up the driveway got bigger, until Rio, who had gone down to the gates to wave people off, was close enough for her to see the grim expression on his face.

He must have seen her because he changed direction and walked up the steps directly into the kitchen.

His face looked as if it were carved of stone, his eyes flat, expressionless and bleak.

She forgot her decision to be cold and distant

the moment he walked in, and just fizzed up. 'If you're going to say it wasn't what it looked like, you can save your breath.'

He arched a sardonic brow and gave her a nasty smile. 'I wasn't.'

'So you admit it, then!' she shrilled out, appalled that he wasn't even showing an iota of shame.

Rio looked at her through narrowed eyes. 'Would it matter if I denied it?' He knew if he did, there would just be the next time and then the time after that, and he would end up spending his life soothing her insecurities, which would eventually ruin, not just her life, but his as well. He had seen how jealousy could poison a relationship and he'd been a fool, he could see that now, to believe that trust might be possible between them.

'I think I deserve an explanation,' she said tightly.

'I think I deserve your trust,' he countered.

'So if you walked in on me with a half-dressed man all over me you'd be just as trusting, would you?' she snapped. 'I thought we might be able to talk this through, but—'

'No, you didn't, you already made up your

mind what happened. Oh, I'm not saying you wouldn't have minded seeing me grovel!' he flung back. 'But even if you saw fit to forgive me, you'd bring it up whenever I got out of line!' By the time he had finished his chest was heaving, and he was visibly shaking with the force of his emotions.

In Gwen's heart there had been a small corner that had secretly wanted him to say something to make her feel less angry, less betrayed. He would say it was all a silly mistake and they'd both laugh over it. She'd wanted him to talk her down from the ledge but he wasn't—if anything, he was pushing her further away.

He didn't just not love her; he actually seemed to despise her.

A block of ice had formed in her chest in the region of her heart and she could not imagine it melting any time soon.

'I think,' she said quietly, 'that Ellie and I should go home.' She gulped and realised she had started to think of this place as home, not because of the beauty and the fine furnishings, but simply because Rio was here too.

'Go?' He looked shocked and then seemed to recover himself. 'Yes, fine. If that's what you want, I'll arrange the flight.'

# CHAPTER TWELVE

As the taxi drew up in front of the cottage she felt none of the comforting sense she had anticipated she'd feel coming home.

'All right, love?'

She blinked and smiled at the driver. 'Fine, thanks.'

'Let me help you with this lot.'

The driver drove away with a generous tip in his pocket and Gwen put her key in the lock. The slight musty smell she had got used to made her nose twitch as she stepped inside, and it felt a lot smaller than she remembered.

She put Ellie down and walked across to a vase of wilted roses that she had missed during her rushed packing. The murky brown water in the bottom explained the smell.

'Right,' she said brightly to Ellie. 'We're home. Isn't that lovely? How cosy. We're going to have a wonderful summer together.'

'Swim?' Ellie said hopefully.

Gwen felt a stab of guilt. Was she being self-ish in taking Ellie away from Rio? Shouldn't she be prepared to compromise to give her daughter the chance of a better life? She glanced out of the window where the gathering grey clouds seemed to echo her mood. It felt as if she were depriving Ellie of a life of sunshine and pools and... Her glance slid to the bin, where dead flower heads pushed at the lid, and she wanted to sit down and cry.

Instead she straightened her shoulders, lifted her chin and halted the creeping guilt and gathering self-pity. Her uncertainty vanished as she decided she had done the right thing—and Rio must have agreed with her because he'd not tried to stop them leaving. In fact he'd facilitated their departure.

Her determined smile was tinged with bitterness but she knew there was more to a happy child than swimming pools.

'I'll blow up the paddling pool,' she told Ellie, who didn't hear. She had tipped out a tub of building blocks and was sitting in the middle of them all, announcing her intention of building a beach house.

Later that afternoon Ellie was down for her nap, meaning it was the perfect time to unpack, but somehow Gwen could not work up the enthusiasm for the task. Instead, remembering her promise, she went to the small shed where a motley collection of garden tools and children's toys were stored.

She found the small plastic paddling pool she had bought during the sales last year, in the optimistic hope that they might have a heatwave before Ellie got too big to fit into it. There was no sign of the foot pump she had bought at the same time.

She took it outside and unfolded it, shaking the dust off it before choosing a spot in the shade of a flowering cherry that was no longer flowering.

Right. She took a deep breath and fitted her lips to one of the valves in the rim—how hard could it be? It wasn't exactly a big paddling pool.

There were reminders everywhere of their recent occupation. The toys, the bright mobile, the smell… Rio wandered into the bedroom where, ridiculously, she had stripped the bed, and found his nostrils flaring at the evocative scent of the light floral soap Gwen used.

*Por Dios!* He strode outside, taking big gulps of fresh air, but somehow the scent of wild thyme on the breeze couldn't get that scent of Gwen out of his nose, or the rest of her out of his head.

He hung onto his anger and reminded himself that he'd done the right thing letting her go, but somehow the statement didn't carry *quite* the same ring of conviction as it so recently had.

She was the one who had talked about trust but when it came down to it, and trust was needed, she had none for him. She hadn't been willing to listen to any explanations.

*Did you even offer her any?*

He frowned darkly at the unhelpful contribution of the voice in his head. She should not have needed any.

*The same way you wouldn't have needed any if the situation had been reversed? Wasn't she right about that? Wouldn't you have gone into full Neanderthal chest-beating mode if you'd seen her alone with a nearly naked man?*

*Doesn't being in love come with some inse-*
*curities and primitive responses?*

His internal dialogue came to an abrupt halt
as a look of amazed realisation spread across
his face. He'd been running away from love
all his life, believing that it was the cause of
his mother's hellish years, but that hadn't been
love, it had been a perversion of it.

Love was the way Gwen looked at Ellie; love
was what he felt when he... He groaned. Had
he just let the best thing in life walk away
from him? No, he had actually arranged the
transport for her, just because he was a coward who thought it was better to be lonely than
take a risk on love, better to be alone than let
history repeat itself.

But Gwen had crept into his heart despite
himself. There, he'd admitted it, even though
he knew it was a mistake to admit, even to
himself, that he wanted a family and love, because admitting it laid you wide open to all
this pain he was feeling right now.

Gwen paused, her head spinning dizzily from
her efforts to inflate the sad-looking paddling
pool. She dropped it and heard the hiss of

air escape, leaving it looking pretty much as she felt.

Tears of self-pity pushed hotly against her eyelids and she blinked.

'You are being totally ridiculous,' she told herself.

'There's a lot of it going about.'

She spun around in the direction of the slow, deep, familiar drawl, her hair following her a second later, heart kicking against her ribcage drawing a loud gasp from her open mouth.

'You...here? How...? Why...?'

'In order: yes, I'm here. How: I chartered a jet because you had mine. And why: because I want to bring you home.'

Her face lost what little colour it had, and the wariness didn't leave her eyes; she was not about to misread this situation. 'You don't have to do that. I'm not going to try and stop you seeing Ellie and I've been thinking about it. The house-next-door thing; I'll do it,' she declared. It would hurt like hell to see his comings and goings with the beautiful women who drifted in and out of his life, and even more horrifying to contemplate the one that might eventually stay there with him. But what right did she have to deprive Ellie of a father as a constant in her life just because Gwen couldn't have him as one in hers?

Some emotion she struggled to interpret flickered in his dark silk-framed eyes. 'You would?'

She nodded. 'So long as she's not exposed to... Er... I mean, I'll need you to keep your private life quite separate from her—that's non-negotiable,' she told him earnestly.

'So no wild orgies in the nursery, then.'

'You know what I mean.' This was hard enough without him mocking her.

'Relax. That offer is no longer on the table.'

Her face fell and she half turned to hide her mortification but a hand on her shoulder pulled her back.

'I don't want a wall between us.' He curved one hand around the side of her face and looked deep into her eyes. 'I don't even want air between us.' He bent down and fitted his mouth to hers. The kiss was deep and hungry and tinged with a tenderness that brought tears to her eyes.

She emerged breathless.

'I know what you're thinking,' he said.

She looked at him with shiny eyes and thought, *That's more than I do!* Her mind was in a whirl and she barely knew if she was sitting or standing, but she was definitely floating, though a voice in her head was still telling her to be cautious.

'I'm not asking you to leave work if you don't want to. We can buy a house near this school. There's a small estate for sale within commuting distance and—'

She lifted a hand to his lips to quiet him for a moment, as her head was reeling. 'Are you asking me to move in with you...' she paused '...for Ellie?'

'No, I'm asking you to move in with me for me,' he said huskily, taking her hand and pressing it to his chest. 'I've a Gwen-sized hole inside me and if you leave me, I'll always feel this way. There was *nothing*,' he emphasised, 'going on that night with Rachel. She was grief-stricken and drunk, and I was cornered and actually relieved to see you.'

'I think I already knew that. I just wanted—'

'To hear me say it,' he completed with a deep sigh. 'And you deserved that.' He lifted both hands to his head and pushed his fingers deep into his hair. 'Just…just be with me, Gwen. I'll try to be the person you need. I swear I will. I love you and I've been trying to pretend I didn't because I was scared…a coward…but I'm not running from love any more. Marry me, Gwen, and be my family.'

By the time he had finished the sobs were shaking her body and tears were running down her cheeks.

'Please tell me that means you're happy,' he begged, wiping away the tears with the pad of his thumb as he bent in to kiss her salty lips.

She nodded. 'It's just I was so miserable and now I'm so happy! Oh, I love you so much, Rio. I think I always did right from that very first time we were together. A lot has changed since then but not that.' She suddenly gave a little laugh of pure joy. 'Is this real? Is it really happening?'

'I know I'm not good enough for you, Gwen, but I promise I'll try to be. You will marry me?'

She nodded, her emotions glowing in her eyes. 'Oh, yes, I'll marry you—and you are good enough for me,' she declared fiercely.

'You're the best man I know and Ellie loves you too.'

He took her hands in his and lifted them to his lips. 'When I think of you being all alone it kills me, giving birth and no one to be there for you. It'll be different next time!'

'Next time?' she echoed.

He searched her face, a shade of concern in his eyes. 'If you want a next time, Gwen. For me, I already have everything I want in you and Ellie.'

'Well, actually, yesterday Ellie was saying she'd like a baby…'

A smile glimmered in his eyes. 'Really?'

'Or a cow.'

He gave a laugh, and she loved the sound.

'I love her but I draw the line at having a cow.'

'She'll be sad but I think she might be happy enough with a baby brother or sister.'

'Or one of each.'

She caught his hands and put them on her hips before stretching up to kiss his mouth. 'It's negotiable, but in the meantime make yourself useful and blow up your daughter's paddling pool.'

He grinned. 'I have a much better use for my breath.'

He absolutely did.

* * * * *

# LET'S TALK

# *Romance*

For exclusive extracts, competitions
and special offers, find us online:

f facebook.com/millsandboon

⊙ @millsandboonuk

𝕏 @millsandboon

Or get in touch on 0844 844 1351*

For all the latest titles coming soon,
visit millsandboon.co.uk/nextmonth

*Calls cost 7p per minute plus your phone company's price per
minute access charge

# Want even more
# ROMANCE?

## Join our bookclub today!

'Mills & Boon books, the perfect way to escape for an hour or so.'

Miss W. Dyer

'Excellent service, promptly delivered and very good subscription choices.'

Miss A. Pearson

'You get fantastic special offers and the chance to get books before they hit the shops'

Mrs V. Hall

**Visit millsandbook.co.uk/Bookclub and save on brand new books.**

## MILLS & BOON